"Welcome to 'Cooking with Jillian.' I'm Jillian Reed—"

"—and I'm Boondock Bill," boomed her assistant in a deep Southern accent. "But you can call me Bubba."

Horrified, Jillian could only stare at the man who had taken a position beside her at the counter. The twang seemed to vibrate from his words.

"Where did you get that microphone?" she demanded.

"An' Miss Jillian here is going to show us how to make some dee-licious Artichoke Soup with hazelnuts and cog-nac."

"That's *cognac.* Now if you'll excuse me, I'd like to proceed."

"Why in tarnation do you always have to cook stuff in some kind of fancy wine? Why not something ordinary, like Beef in Beer?"

Camera One had zoomed in on Bill's innocent grin, and the camera crew could barely contain their laughter.

"Cut!" Jillian proclaimed to the rolling cameras. "Can someone get him out of here and find me a sane assistant?"

Dear Reader,

It's a brand-new year, and we at Silhouette Romance have a brand-new lineup of dashing heroes, winsome heroines and happy endings galore! Winter is the perfect season to curl up and read—you provide the hot cocoa, and we'll provide the good books!

We're proud to launch our new FABULOUS FATHERS series this month with Diana Palmer's *Emmett*. Each month, we'll feature a different hero in a heartwarming story about fatherhood. *Emmett* is a special book from a favorite author in more ways than one—it's Diana Palmer's fiftieth Silhouette novel, and it's part of the LONG, TALL TEXANS series, too!

This month, Stella Bagwell's HEARTLAND HOLIDAYS trilogy is completed with *New Year's Baby*. It's a truly emotional tale that brings the Gallagher clan's story to a satisfying conclusion.

Rounding out the month, we have Geeta Kingsley's *The Old-Fashioned Way*, Carolyn Monroe's *A Lovin' Spoonful,* Jude Randal's *Northern Manhunt,* and an inspiring romance from first-time Silhouette author Jeanne Rose, entitled *Believing in Angels*.

In the months to come, watch for Silhouette Romance titles by many of your favorite authors, including Annette Broadrick, Elizabeth August and Marie Ferrarella.

Here's to a sparkling New Year!

Anne Canadeo
Senior Editor
Silhouette Romance

A LOVIN' SPOONFUL
Carolyn Monroe

Published by Silhouette Books New York

America's Publisher of Contemporary Romance

To Peggy Greene, who actually thinks cooking is fun, and to the memory of Floyd "Pop" Greene, Sr. With special thanks to Larry Bly and Laban Johnson, of *Cookin' Cheap,* for inspiring me to write this book; to WRLH-TV and WCVE-TV for tours of their stations; to Sandra Jones for sharing her expertise; and to Danny and Fay Henderson, the ultimate cute couple.

SILHOUETTE BOOKS
300 E. 42nd St., New York, N.Y. 10017

A LOVIN' SPOONFUL

Copyright © 1993 by Carolyn Greene

ISBN: 0-373-08912-0

First Silhouette Books printing January 1993

Printed in the U.S.A.

Books by Carolyn Monroe

Silhouette Romance

Kiss of Bliss #847
A Lovin' Spoonful #912

CAROLYN MONROE

lives within spitting distance of Flat Rock in Powhatan, Virginia, with her firefighter husband and two terrific children. Carolyn used to write feature articles for the local newspaper; she now prefers fiction to nonfiction because she can make up the facts. She has received awards for her writing, but better than that, she has received checks. Carolyn is a member of Romance Writers of America and the Virginia Romance Writers.

BOONDOCK BILL'S BEEF IN BEER

2 carrots, chopped
2 celery stalks, chopped
5 large mushrooms, chopped
2 onions, chopped
1½ lbs beef tips or ground beef
flour
⅓ cup beer
3 tbsp ketchup
cooked egg noodles or rice (optional)

Heat oven to 350° F. Sauté carrots, celery, mushrooms and onions. Add salt and pepper to taste. Remove mixture to casserole dish.

Roll beef in flour, and brown in a lightly oiled pan. Spoon beef onto vegetables.

In a cup or small bowl, combine beer and ketchup. Pour over beef and vegetables. While waiting one hour for it to bake, finish off what's left in the beer can.

Dish it out as is or over egg noodles or rice. Feeds 4 normal people, but Memphis and I can put it away by ourselves!

Chapter One

She was doing it again.

Bill Clayton turned up the volume on his headset and watched the monitors in the master-control booth. He cringed when her voice quaked. To make matters worse, she used "and uh" too often while describing the next step in the intricate recipe she demonstrated for the television audience.

She was flubbing up royally. Bill could almost hear the channels clicking as he imagined viewers tuning in to competing stations.

Competing stations, indeed! He leaned back in the swivel chair and propped his sneakers on the corner of the console. The difference between his station's ratings and the others' was laughable. To everyone but him, that was.

Bill glanced over at his best friend and investor to find him beaming at the televised image of the lovely, tongue-tied brunette.

"Why did you do this to me?" Bill asked the burly man sprawled in a chair in the corner.

Memphis Reason grudgingly took his eyes off the monitor. "Ain't she the prettiest little thing you ever did see?" He rubbed the back of his tattooed forearm across his graying beard.

Bill had to agree with his friend. With her dark hair and classic features, she reminded him of a young Elizabeth Taylor, only warmer and more vulnerable. Much more vulnerable. She was enough to bring out the protective instincts in a man.

"But don't let my wife know I said that," said Memphis. "She thinks *you* hired her, you ol' rascal."

"What about talent?" Bill swept a hand toward the viewing screen. "You can't make ratings go up just by putting a babe in front of the camera."

"Hey, man, she's got plenty of talent. Why, look at that fancy stuff she's pulling out of the oven." Both men leaned forward to try to identify the unusual dish. "Nobody I know can cook anything that fancy."

"Bingo."

Bill put his feet back on the floor. He'd better go back to his office and start clearing his desk. Might as well try to look professional when he called her into his office.

He'd fired people before, but he never liked it. This time he hated it more than ever.

"That's all for today." The brunette smiled becomingly at the camera's red blinking light as she displayed her latest culinary creation. "I'm Jillian Reed. Be sure to tune in tomorrow for more 'Cooking With Jillian.'"

The spotlights dimmed, and the show was over. Jillian set down the plate of coq au vin and sagged against the counter.

What was wrong with her? Why couldn't she talk her way through a relatively simple recipe without stumbling over her own tongue? It wasn't as if she hadn't made the chicken-in-wine dish a thousand times before. Normally Jillian felt very much in control. She'd been cooking ever since she was big enough to stand on a stool at her grandmother's elbow. Plus, she'd been teaching cooking since she'd earned her chef's diploma a few years ago.

There was no reason for her jitters. She hadn't even been this nervous when, as a teenager, she'd prepared meals to help her father impress his Army superiors. Nor had her knees shaken when she'd cooked exotic banquet dinners for her ex-husband Quint's law associates.

"You okay, Miss Reed?"

Jillian looked up to see the cameraman watching her as he put the cameras and cords back in place. Mike was such a nice, quiet man, she was tempted to confess her feelings of inadequacy. She caught herself. Like a whisper, she could almost hear her father's voice: "Never reveal a lack of confidence, especially to the troops."

With the studio lights lowered and the set lights on, she hadn't been able to see the crew's reaction to her show. Right now, she wasn't sure she wanted to know what they thought of her performance.

"Yes, thank you, Mike. Just tired, that's all."

It was bad enough that she would have to discuss with Darlene, the show's editor, how to compensate for her on-air flop—but, to the rest of the staff, she must maintain a professional distance. It wouldn't do to let them know how stupid she felt talking to a camera. It sure would have made matters easier to have seen a dozen eager cooking students waiting for her next instruction.

Jillian straightened and started collecting the assorted dishes and utensils used during the show. She put them in the sink behind the island counter and rolled up her sleeves. If she raised a fuss, she might persuade the owners of this tiny television station to assign one of the other employees to wash the dishes, but the warm suds on her hands helped ease the tension until her shoulders relaxed from their stiffened position.

Darlene bounced onto the seat and helped herself to a piece of chicken. "Mmm," she said, forking in another mouthful before she finished chewing the first. "What are you going to do with the rest of this stuff?"

"I'm sending it home with you." Jillian hesitated a couple of seconds until Mike finished coiling the cable around his hand and elbow and then left. "You're going to earn your supper with all the cutting you'll have to do on today's taping."

"No offense, but this is a half-hour show, not fifteen minutes," Darlene blurted after she swallowed the last bite.

Jillian stopped wiping the pan. The woman might have more television experience, but Jillian's confidence level didn't need the additional bashing. The hurt look she sent the younger woman had Darlene apologizing for the slur.

"Sorry, I didn't mean that." Darlene reached into the refrigerator for a soda to wash down her hastily eaten lunch. "You'll get the hang of things," she assured her. "Give yourself time. You've only been at it for two weeks."

Two weeks, and she'd gotten worse, not better. At this rate, she'd be drooling and babbling by the end of the month.

"By the way…" Darlene emitted a carbonated burp, and Jillian blinked at her crudeness. Darlene laughed at her reaction and continued. "Mr. Clayton wants to see you when you're done here."

Mr. Clayton? Jillian wondered why he wanted to see her. The big, bearded one that looked like a motorcycle gang member had been the one to hire her. Bill Clayton had never said more than hello in passing.

Actually he'd said, "G'mawnin'," in that southwest Virginia accent of his. Having spent several years studying the French language to complement her French cuisine lessons, she now found her employer's southern accent almost comedic—in an odd sort of way. Despite his manner of speaking, or maybe because of it, he still managed to exude an effortless male confidence that made people pay attention when he spoke.

Mr. Reason's dialect sounded even more twangy than Mr. Clayton's but, oddly, it didn't bother her. Maybe it was because she would expect a man who looked like Memphis Reason to speak in a backwoods drawl. But Bill Clayton, except for his casual attire, seemed to have otherwise left behind his rural upbringing. It came as a shock whenever she heard that funny voice come out of such an attractive man. And his laugh. It carried all the way to her office. Unrestrained and infectious, his was often joined by the others.

Jerking her mind back to the present and away from thoughts of her boss's attractiveness, Jillian rinsed the last dish and dried her hands on the dish towel before turning back to Darlene.

"Did Boondock Bill say what he wanted?"

Immediately Jillian regretted her indiscretion. Darlene's mouth dropped open and her hand flew up to cover it. Then she let out a little squeal of delight.

"I love it, I love it!" Darlene exclaimed. "That nickname fits him perfectly. Wait'll I tell the others."

Jillian laid a restraining hand on the program editor's arm. "I wish you wouldn't let it get around. Mr. Clayton is our employer, and I shouldn't have called him that."

Darlene had turned away and was heading for the exit when she said over her shoulder, "Lighten, up Jill. He'll probably laugh as hard as the next guy. Anyone who could start his own chain of video rental stores against the bank's advice and then sell it at the profit he got is used to having the last laugh." The door clicked shut behind Darlene.

"It's *Jillian,*" she muttered to the empty set.

Grabbing the dishcloth, Jillian started cleaning the counter with a vengeance.

After years of learning to say just the right thing at just the right time, she'd opened her big mouth and neatly inserted both feet. Jillian only hoped Darlene was mature enough not to spread the unbecoming nickname around the station.

Fat chance.

Jillian hung the dishcloth on the rod over the sink and went to her office to prepare for her meeting with Bill Clayton.

The office was small and located in a remote corner of the station—Jillian suspected it had once been a janitor's closet—but the walls on one side of the room were conveniently lined with shelves. The shelves now held dozens of recipe boxes and cookbooks, six years' worth of her favorite *Bon Appetit* magazines, and a small television and tape machine for viewing her shows before they aired.

Jillian rummaged through folders on her desk until she located the one with next week's scripts. Certain that Bill Clayton intended to discuss her program plans, she wanted to be prepared.

She opened the folder and picked up the top sheet. The paper shook in her hands. With a start, she realized she was nervous about this meeting with her employer. Although her culinary skills were unquestionable, Jillian knew without a doubt that her on-air performance left a lot to be desired. She'd always had difficulty letting go, and she'd always envied people who had the ability to make everything they did seem fun.

Except for the cooking classes she'd taught at a community college, Jillian had never been comfortable in a crowd. In fact, that was one of the reasons she'd taken up cooking as a hobby, then later as a career pursuit. Whereas other teenage girls might have squelched their loneliness and insecurity by eating double-Dutch chocolate cake and second helpings of linguine, Jillian had squelched hers by creating the richest chocolate cakes imaginable and experimenting with clam sauces until hers was the creamiest.

Cooking had been a solitary diversion, and even more so after her father's military career had taken them away from her grandmother's neighborhood in Houston. She couldn't pack her few, close friends into the crates when her family moved every other year, but no matter where her father was stationed, a stove and refrigerator were certain to welcome her into her new home.

Jillian had been halfway through her freshman year in high school when her father had accepted a promotion to the Pentagon. It was in her senior year in the Arlington, Virginia, high school that Jillian had penned her aspirations for the yearbook: *I will earn my chef's diploma and become a household name by the time I'm thirty.* It was also in Northern Virginia that she had met Quint and given up her dream of becoming a famous chef, at least for the duration of their short, ill-fated marriage.

Now, with six months left before her thirtieth birthday, she realized her lofty goal would be almost impossible to reach. Maybe, she consoled herself, she should give herself an extra three years for the time she'd wasted with Quint.

Unbidden, a memory of her tenth-year high school reunion pushed its way into her mind. It had been just a year and a half ago, but it seemed more like a lifetime. Quint had escorted her to the reunion, and they'd separated a couple of months afterward. As she and her former classmates had sat around examining their yearbooks, Karen, who had been Jillian's partner in science lab, cruelly ribbed her about her career goal.

"Looks like you won't make it," Karen had teased loud enough for everyone to hear. "But it seems the class knew you better than you knew yourself," she said, pointing to the prediction printed next to her picture. Jillian gritted her teeth as she remembered the laughter that followed Karen's reading out loud that she had veen voted "Most Likely to Get Married."

Well, they may have been right on that account, but Jillian was determined to become at least half as successful as her idol, Julia Child. And she had vehemently told them so.

Her determination was doubly potent after the way Quint had battered her self-esteem with his womanizing ways. To divert the blame from himself, he'd frequently belittled her, criticizing her slightest mistakes. To prove him wrong, she had tried to be perfect in everything she did. She made sure that her appearance was flawless, her housekeeping was spotless and her meals and parties were unequaled. No matter how hard she tried to give Quint nothing to find fault about, he always managed to make her feel incompetent, and frequently said as much.

It later became a point of honor to prove to herself that she could reach her goal, despite what he said.

"Cooking With Jillian" was her vehicle to success. With any luck—and it would take a lot for Jillian to overcome her stage fright—the show would become syndicated. Then, with a sure audience, she could publish a cookbook.

Now all she had to do was make the show successful enough to be syndicated.

Jillian reached for a pencil to make a note on her script, but her trembling hand hit the cup and sent pens scattering across the floor. *Take a deep breath,* she told herself. *Try to forget your future is riding on this show.*

She closed her eyes and took another deep breath before dropping to her knees on the thinly carpeted floor. She gathered up the pencils and pens and reached for a stray that had rolled under the desk.

Bill's steps automatically slowed as he approached Jillian Reed's office. His fingers tightened around the newspaper in his hand. He hated what he was about to do but he hated what he'd read in the paper even more. Something had to be done. Immediately.

Bill stepped into her office and stopped cold in his tracks. Her posterior aimed skyward and the upper half of her body wedged under her desk, she caused his thoughts to veer crazily and his blood pressure to skyrocket.

He stood rooted to the spot while he waited for her to notice him. In the meantime, he feasted on the view of her nicely rounded bottom straining against the soft T-shirt-type fabric of her dress. He smiled as he realized this was the first time he'd seen Ms. Reed looking less than regal.

"Mmm," he said, "rump roast."

The lovely Ms. Reed jerked, cracked her head against the underside of her desk, and said words his mama had washed his mouth out with soap for saying.

Immediately Bill went to her and knelt beside her. "Are you all right?" He cradled her between his legs as his hands swept through the long, velvety brown hair in search of a cut or lump on her scalp. Bill breathed a sigh of relief to know that she hadn't injured her beautiful head.

The smell of her intoxicated him, and he barely heeded the fact that his fingers now twined aimlessly in the dark strands. In the next moment, she turned to face him and he became lost in the pale blue eyes that stared back at him.

Rimmed with thick, black lashes, her eyes elevated her from a classic beauty to an extraordinary one. His gaze took in the small nose with the slightly flared nostrils that made him picture a thoroughbred mare testing the wind for danger. And then down to her lips, soft and lush, but not quite full enough to hide the crooked eyetooth that seemed to be her sole imperfection.

Bill's chest constricted until he could barely draw a breath. His perusal of her had lasted no more than a few seconds, but it was long enough for his body's self-defense mechanism to kick in. It was as if his body knew, when his mind did not, that her own special fragrance was as potent as a deadly drug.

It certainly took its toll on him. Why else would he be so disoriented in her presence when, from a distance, he had merely appreciated her looks as much as any other healthy male would?

Jillian blinked twice, stunned at the effect this man had on her. Why was she so attracted to him? She knew that behind that thick mountain accent there existed a keen intelligence. But he was not the type of man she ordinarily found herself attracted to.

Quint had courted her with expensive trinkets, the best wines and food, and pretty words that accomplished what he wanted. That's what she was used to.

This man, on the other hand, compared portions of her anatomy to a cut of beef.

Belatedly she realized she'd rested her forearm intimately against his muscular thigh while he'd caressed her hair in that odd, quiet way of his. She lifted her arm in the same slow, even motion she would have used if handling nitroglycerin.

Even after years of acting the part of a cool, self-assured young woman, the role didn't seem natural to her. One day, she feared, someone would find out that her air of reserve and sophistication was just that—an act. And for some reason, her act didn't seem effective on Bill Clayton. Something told her to be especially careful around him. Otherwise he might be the one to find her out.

Jillian started to rise, but he beat her to it and extended a hand to assist her. With a comfortable distance between them, she casually ran a hand over her mussed hair and shook the wrinkles from her dress. Assured that she once again looked the part of a professional businesswoman, she straightened her posture and stepped away. It wouldn't do to melt all over her employer merely because he showed a bit of human compassion.

"I'm sorry I startled you," he said, taking a step toward her.

Jillian backed up one step equal to his own. "I'm fine." She'd meant it to come out sounding confident, but her words were clipped.

Bill Clayton's eyes narrowed accordingly. His lips pressed together in a thin line, making Jillian aware of the spot his razor missed in the shallow cleft of his chin.

"Excuse me, Ms. Reed. I guess I was acting friendlier than a wet bird dog. Please accept my apology."

Jillian rested a hand on her hip. Was he teasing her? His intense gray-green eyes said no.

She'd give him the benefit of the doubt. "No apology is necessary, Mr. Clayton. I appreciate your concern." She turned to her desk and picked up the script folder. "I was just getting together some information to come and see you when my pencil cup overturned."

"Yes, well . . ." He tapped the newspaper against the palm of his hand, then set it on her desk. "This is what I wanted to see you about."

The morning paper had been folded open to the entertainment section. Jillian knew before she read the short, terse article that it would not be flattering. The look on Bill's face told her so.

...Miss Reed's on-air personality is as boring as her recipes are complex. If "Cooking With Jillian" is an indication of WXYZ's programming under new ownership, then viewers would do better to tune in to "The Bold and the Heartless" to see what Ina and Sam are cooking up.

An article about "Cooking With Jillian" does not, in all conscience, belong on the entertainment page; however, my editor wouldn't let me put it in the obituary column.

Willing away the tears that burned at the corners of her eyes, Jillian picked up her scissors and began clipping the column. In the past, when her best hadn't been good enough, she had steeled her determination and tried to do better. And though the reviewer's criticisms had stung, she resolved to try again.

She hadn't cried when Quint had left her for another woman. She certainly wouldn't cry now over some stupid job—even if that job was the key to her life's dream. She'd show that reporter how wrong he was. And she'd do it within six months—before her thirtieth birthday.

"You're not going to keep that, are you?"

"Of course. It's a baseline for improvement."

Bill watched as she taped the clipping to a sheet of paper, hit it with the hole puncher, and inserted the damning article into a three-ring binder. He had to admire her gumption.

Her acting, however, left a lot to be desired. Although she tried to cover her disappointment with a stiff back and matter-of-fact attitude, he could tell the review had cut her to slivers inside. Knowing this made him pause before he gave her the ax. But no matter how much he ached for her—no matter how attractive and desirable he found her—he had a station to run. Preferably a successful one. Without a doubt, the station's image would improve with the cancellation of Jillian's show.

"Jillian, I think it's admirable that you want to improve." He jerked his eyes away from her and started pacing in front of her desk. "Unfortunately time is a luxury I can't give you. Your show is being canceled."

There, he'd done it. Maybe in a few months or a year, he'd forget the way Jillian's mouth dropped open for a split second before she gathered her composure. He hoped she wouldn't cry or, worse, beg him for another chance.

"You can't do that!"

"I can't do wha—"

"You can't just cancel my show without giving me a fair chance. It's only been two weeks. I suggest you think about this some more before you make a final decision, Mr. Clayton."

Now it was Bill's turn to stand with his mouth open. A pounding headache hammered in his right temple, and he tried to rub it away. He pushed aside some folders and sat wearily on the corner of her desk. Jillian continued standing, her chin raised defiantly.

"Miss Reed, you're new to television, so maybe you're not aware of some of the basics. First, most stations don't hire somebody before seeing a demo tape."

"Mr. Reason didn't ask for one."

"Well, technically, he shouldn't have been hiring anyone."

"But he said he's your partner."

Bill clenched his teeth. It was bad enough that he had to fire the woman. He had no desire to open another sensitive subject and discuss his business partnership with her. Bill was grateful to his best friend for putting up his trucking company as collateral so Bill could start his first business, a video rental store. The store had bucked the predictions of his banker, going on to become one of the leading video rental franchises in the state. So when his best friend had expressed an interest in investing in the television-station venture, Bill couldn't say no. However, he hadn't expected Memphis to meddle so much in it.

"Second," he continued as if she hadn't interrupted, "WXYZ's success depends on its ratings. And since your cooking show is not pulling in its share of ratings, we're going to have to try something else."

As much as he would have liked for her program to be a success, he couldn't waste any more airtime on her.

Unfortunately she wouldn't take no for an answer.

Jillian struggled to control her anger and disappointment. He had no right to do this to her. She ought to just push his nonchalant rear right off her desk!

He spared her the temptation when he got up and started prowling the room again.

"Mr. Clayton, ratings weren't a condition of my employment." She took brief satisfaction that her anger hadn't made her voice quiver. "If you cancel my show now, you'll be guilty of breach of contract."

He stopped flipping through a cookbook and turned around to face her. "You don't have a contract."

True, she'd never signed a formal document, but wasn't a verbal offer an implied contract? Jillian was about to say so when he stepped closer to show her a recipe in her *Down Home Cookin'* cookbook.

She tried not to notice how his arm brushed hers. She tried even harder not to wish the touch had been intentional. She consciously pushed her traitorous thoughts aside in order to concentrate on the issue at hand—her job.

Bill had gone back to browsing through the book. "Now, this is the kind of food I'm used to eating. Have you ever considered demonstrating spoonbread or stewed tomatoes instead of those highfalutin' dishes most people can't even pronounce?"

With exaggerated patience, Jillian took the book out of his hands and stepped past him to replace it on the shelf. "This book was given to me as a *joke.*"

"I don't get it."

Jillian paused as she considered this revelation. With an amused laugh, she said, "I'm not surprised."

Either he ignored the teasing jibe, or he didn't get that, either. "What I'm trying to say, Jillian—"

Jillian involuntarily ground her teeth when her name came out sounding like *Jill-yen.*

"—is that you might do better featuring easier recipes. Take those church cookbooks, for example. They have real recipes that are used by real people. Maybe if you thought more commercially, the show would have a better chance."

He was giving her another opportunity! Unfortunately he had soured the moment by using the *C* word. Jillian considered her cooking an art form. If she'd wanted to go the commercial route, she'd have opened a hamburger stand.

It was no use trying to explain her feelings to him or to explain that what he described as fancy cooking could be everyday fare if only she was allowed to teach the viewers some of the tricks of the trade. Like many others, Bill carried the common misconception that elegant cooking was difficult cooking. It would be almost impossible to make him understand that she *could* pull off the kind of show she had in mind.

Instead she must take advantage of his change of heart.

"Give me six months, and 'Cooking With Jillian' will be a household phrase."

Bill shoved his hands into his pockets and rocked back on his heels as he watched her determination grow. Too bad she wasn't as talented as she was beautiful. Sometimes, as he well knew, determination and sheer persistence compensated for a lack of raw talent.

He would probably live to regret his impulsive decision.

"Six weeks. But if the ratings aren't up by then, you're out on your keister."

Chapter Two

Bill felt like a spy, watching her again from the control room as she prepared for taping. He kept telling himself that he was merely taking a professional interest in Jillian and her program. She had mentioned she'd be trying something new. As owner and manager, he was obliged to keep up with the station's activities.

At least, that's what he told Memphis when his friend predictably found him here.

He sat back to watch the screened images of Jillian. He had to admit, from both camera angles she looked good. Delectable, even. He smiled at his own pun.

Darlene stepped onto the set, and the two women began an animated conversation.

Bill reached over and tapped the program director's headset. "What's the matter?" he asked.

"Jillian's assistant didn't show up."

Memphis piped in, "Why don't you go help her, Bill? Didn't you learn a little about cooking in your parents' diner?"

Bill let out an exasperated sigh. "Don't you have a truck to drive?"

"I'd rather watch her."

"You and only a handful of others in all of Richmond," Bill muttered. He got up and walked to the studio.

"Darlene," Jillian persisted, "please find somebody. I don't care who it is, as long as they know the difference between celery and potatoes."

Bill stepped onto the set and helped himself to a clean dish towel. "I suppose I could give you a hand." He tucked the cloth into his waistband to form a makeshift apron.

Suddenly Jillian realized she *did* care who assisted her. If she'd been nervous and tongue-tied the previous two weeks, Jillian felt absolutely frozen now. Logically she knew he watched her show everyday. She could deal with that. But to have him here on the set while she tried her best to appear calm and poised in front of those merciless cameras was more than she could handle.

"That's very kind of you, Mr. Clayton, but I wouldn't want to disturb your busy schedule." She turned back to Darlene. "Perhaps that college intern in the traffic department could spare a couple of hours."

"Never mind, Darlene. Everything's under control here."

Jillian rankled as he shot her a little grin of victory. "Fine," she conceded. "But just remember to stay off camera."

He smiled again. "You're the boss."

Maybe, she hoped, he'd blend into the background. Even as the thought flitted through her mind, she knew that no matter where the man happened to be, he'd be the focus of attention. To put it gently, he was...different. He was unlike any man she'd ever met before, and she didn't know quite how to deal with him.

In a matter of minutes, the cameras started rolling. It wasn't until after Bill insisted the house lights be turned up that Jillian realized how isolated she'd felt when all else had been shrouded in shadows. Maybe, with different lighting and a few classes in public speaking, she'd settle right into her role as a television show host.

"Welcome to 'Cooking With Jillian,'" she began with more assurance than she'd felt in the past two weeks. "I'm Jillian Reed—"

"And I'm Boondock Bill," boomed her assistant in a deep, southern accent. "But you can call me Bubba."

Horrified, Jillian could only stare at the man who had taken a position beside her at the counter. Today the twang seemed to vibrate from his words. She could swear he was *flaunting* his accent.

"Where did you get that microphone?" she demanded.

"An' Miss Jillian here is gonna show us how to make some dee-licious artichoke soup with hazelnuts and cog-nac."

"That's *cognac*. Now if you'll excuse me, I'd like to proceed."

"Why in tarnation do you always have to cook stuff in some kind of fancy wine? Why don't you try something ordinary like Beef in Beer?"

A glance at the monitor showed Camera One had zoomed in on Bill's innocently grinning visage. And with the house lights up, it was plain to see the camera crew could barely contain their laughter over their boss's unusual behavior.

Jillian teed her hands to signal time out. "Cut," she proclaimed to the rolling cameras. "Darlene, would you get him out of here and find me a sane assistant?"

"That's not necessary," Bill said, his demeanor suddenly contrite. "I'll behave."

His promise lasted about five minutes.

"Next, we'll need four cups of chicken stock," Jillian instructed him as she went on to the next step in the recipe. "While he's measuring the broth, I'll drain the artichoke hearts."

Cabinet doors slammed and in the next instant the grinding of an electric can opener filled the set. Jillian felt a muscle throb at her temple.

Grabbing his hands in both of hers, she exclaimed through clenched teeth, "We do *not* use canned ingredients. The broth . . . is on . . . the stove!"

The show was ruined. She'd have to wait until he left the set, then start all over from the beginning. Why did he have to make things more difficult for her?

Bill shrugged his shoulders and reached for the saucepan. "Don't have a hissy-fit, hon. It just seems like a waste to cook an entire chicken just to use the juice from it. By the way, who's paying for all that stuff you're using?"

After a while, Jillian gritted her teeth and said through a forced smile, "The chicken will be used in the next show."

Jillian gave up the idea that this taping would be used for Friday's show. *If you can't beat them,* she thought, *join then.* Once she relaxed and stopped thinking about having to retape the show, she started to have fun.

Sure, it was a waste of time going through the motions of finishing the show, but she'd heard about the creative personalities in television and how they needed to let off steam occasionally. Maybe that was what Bill Clayton was doing. She'd go along with it for now and consider it her initiation into showbiz. Then, after Bill had gotten the playfulness out of his system, she'd do the show properly with another helper—one less inclined toward hamming it up.

Bill turned out to be a pretty good assistant once she stopped trying to rein him in. With a little clowning, a little cognac, and a lot of fun, they finished making the soup.

Jillian surprised herself by wishing the recipe had a few more steps for them to demonstrate. She really hated for their time together to end.

After rewarming the soup, she ladled the liquid into a bowl and handed it to Bill. Judging from his expression, Jillian knew she'd have more luck getting a four-year-old to try creamed peas.

"For Pete's sake, just try the stuff!"

"Who's Pete?" Bill quipped before she managed to shove a spoonful of the stuff into his mouth. After his initial surprise, he rolled it around on his tongue as if he were sampling a new wine.

Jillian found herself smiling and eagerly waiting for his response. Not that his beef-in-beer taste buds could appreciate good cooking. Nevertheless she wanted his approval, and for reasons beyond job security.

A droplet of soup clung to the corner of his mouth. Before she thought twice about it, she reached up and wiped it away. The touch was brief, but much more intimate than she felt comfortable with. The shadow that passed over Bill's charcoal-and-green eyes revealed that he felt it, too, and he returned a soul-searching gaze. Jillian felt almost naked beneath his assessment, but not embarrassingly so. Openly they studied each other for what seemed like minutes or even hours. In actuality, it was probably only a few seconds.

His face wasn't handsome in the typical sense. In fact, a person might not think him especially good-looking after only the first appraisal. Prominent eyebrows framed a large, masculine nose, and he was so tall he might appear gangly if not for the confident way in which he carried himself.

It wasn't until after the second or third time she'd seen him that she noticed the sensitive gray-green eyes, the high cheekbones, and the long, lean line of his jaw. And the thick, sandy brown hair that touched his collar in the back begged her to brush it away from his face.

Darlene's voice broke into their reverie. "Okay, you two, this is only a half-hour show."

Like a door slamming shut, Bill's eyes shuttered closed. As if nothing had just passed between them, he once again donned his infuriating hillbilly act and pasted on a lopsided grin.

"Wal', goll-lee, Miss Jillian. That there stuff ain't half as bad as it looks!"

And to think that, for the briefest of moments, she'd thought there might be something interesting under that rough exterior.

Jillian turned her attention back to Darlene. "That's a wrap for today."

Bill waved at the camera. "Bye, y'all. Be sure to tune in tomorrow for some more of Miss Jillian's *fine* cookin'."

* * *

As Jillian walked through the reception area and headed for her office, the receptionist handed her a stack of pink telephone messages.

"More phone calls?"

"There's a bigger batch on your desk. I had to empty my message rack twice." The phone rang again. Cindy reached for it and hesitated. "Congratulations on that nice write-up in this morning's paper."

Jillian smiled her thanks and beat a hasty retreat to her office. She supposed she shouldn't complain—the public response to her program was exactly what she'd been hoping for—yet she never imagined it would happen like this.

If she was a suspicious person, she would wonder if Bill or Darlene had switched the tapes on purpose. Jillian had redone the show later that day. As luck would have it, her stage fright had returned in full force, but at least her version was more dignified.

Unfortunately the segment with "Boondock Bill" ended up on the air.

Plopping into her chair, she placed the newspaper by the binder that contained the previous scathing review and started sifting through the telephone messages.

Wants recipe for Beef in Beer.

Loved Boondock Bill. Please bring him back.

Laughed harder than she has in years.

Wants to know how long you two have been married.

And so on. A few were less than kind. One caller even suggested that Jillian's corset strings were too tight and that she should do the public a favor and bring Bill back on the show.

"Over my dead body." Jillian crumpled the offending slip of paper and tossed it into the trash can.

For a moment, she gave in to a wave of self-pity and considered giving up her goal of trying to be a success by the time her thirtieth birthday rolled around. But she'd given up her dream when she married Quint.

She'd given up a lot when she'd married Quint...mostly her confidence. He had torn that to shreds with his constant criticisms. If only she'd known then that his verbal abuse had only been a ploy to mask the fact that he was seeing other women. Maybe, if she'd been able to see past his deceit, her self-image wouldn't have been so shaken. Now, pursuing the goal she'd abandoned upon marrying Quint seemed to be the way to rebuild her confidence. Jillian would prove to herself, if no one else, that she could be a success.

She knew she couldn't let another man come between her and her goal.

With renewed determination, she started planning her next show.

Jillian took a deep breath and pushed upward on the weighted bar. This exercise room was what had sold her on renting the apartment in western Chesterfield County. In the weeks since she'd started her new job at WXYZ, she'd come here often, pumping out her frustration on the weight machines.

Lying on the padded bench, Jillian felt moisture bead on her forehead. Just a few more presses and she'd call it quits for tonight.

From the corner of her eye, she saw someone enter the room. It was a good thing she was almost done, because she hated having an audience while she worked out.

Bill had to look twice before he recognized the brunette under the heavy barbell. Clad in electric-blue, body-clinging stretch tights—or whatever they called those things—and her hair pulled back in a casual ponytail, she held little resemblance to the quiet, businesslike woman at the station. No, the refined woman at the station wouldn't let anyone hear those little grunts of exertion. And although the clothes she usually wore to work were quite feminine, they gave little indication of the exotic curves that now strained against the shiny blue fabric.

Having been raised in the mountains of southwest Virginia, Bill fully appreciated the spectacular view of hills and valleys that Jillian unknowingly offered him. She was making it even harder for him to work up the nerve to have that "little talk" with her. He took the bar from her and set it in its cradle.

Jillian sat up to face him. "What are you doing here?"

Besides ogling you? Bill jerked his attention back to the reason for his after-hours visit. He shoved his hands into his back pockets, remembered his mother's lectures about ripping the seams, and removed them again. "We need to talk."

She leveled a curious gaze at him. "Is it about my job?"

Bill nodded.

"Let me cool down first, then we can go back to my apartment."

Bill walked to the back of the room and sat astride a one-wheeled bike, an excellent vantage point for watching Jillian's slow, fluid motions.

She looked up at him from the floor mat, bashfulness overcoming her. "You're watching."

He grinned. "I can't help it. I'm only human."

"I wish you wouldn't. It makes me feel weird." Weird was hardly the word for how she felt right now, Jillian realized. She'd noticed men watching as she exercised on other occasions. Then, she'd felt like the star of a peep show, as if she'd been undressed with their eyes. That was why she'd chosen this time of evening to work out, when everyone seemed to have something else to do.

And although Bill watched her just as intently, maybe more so, his gaze seemed more admiring than lecherous. Perhaps that was why it seemed even more unsettling than the others.

"There's no need to be shy—I don't have a camera." For effect, he pulled the white lining from his pants pockets.

Jillian answered with a little sigh.

Before she could protest further, he sat beside her on the mat.

"So, how do you do a cool-down?"

Soon they were stretching and breathing in sync. It was all Jillian could do not to stare at the way Bill's slacks flowed over his thick-muscled legs. She supposed he must have gotten lots of exercise walking up and down the mountainside in his home town. She surprised herself by enjoying his company, even though her gut instinct told her he brought bad news.

At work she'd avoided contact with him as much as possible, hoping to forestall the day of reckoning. Almost a month had passed since he'd given her six weeks to prove herself on "Cooking With Jillian." And, quite honestly, she knew she was failing miserably.

On the short walk back to her apartment, the mood grew pensive.

While Jillian showered and changed, Bill wandered around the sparsely decorated living room. Just like her cooking set and her office, the room was stripped of all clutter. Not even a magazine dared grace the polished coffee table. The magazines and books were arranged neatly—and alphabetically, he noticed—on a small bookshelf separating the living room from the dining area. A place for everything, and everything in its place.

Bill's mother lived by that motto, too, but she'd always made a place for niceties such as lace doilies on the easy chair and the generations-old quilt that covered a burn mark his younger sister had left in the sofa when trying her first cigarette. And the crayoned picture that won Bill a first-grade coloring contest held its own place of honor in a frame on the fireplace mantel in his parents' house.

No, there didn't seem to be a place for sentimentalities in this room. Although it was clean and stylish, it didn't give the impression that someone actually lived here.

Jillian emerged from the bathroom looking as spotless as the living room. Her long brown hair, normally pulled back in a fashionable twist, had been released from its ponytail of a few minutes ago and now hung damply around her shoulders. She wore no makeup, but she didn't need to. Her skin glowed from the hot shower, and dark lashes framed vivid blue eyes that squarely met his gaze. Her only hint of nervousness was running the tip of her tongue over her pink lower lip.

For a moment, Bill wished it was his lip she was caressing like that. Quickly leashing his errant thoughts, he pulled his mind back to the matter at hand.

Firing Jillian.

"Would you like some espresso?" It was the proper thing to do, offering him a cup of the strong, black brew, but Jillian was still thankful that doing so served a double purpose of delaying the inevitable.

"No thanks, but do you have any coffee?"

Jillian started to laugh at his joke, but stopped when she noticed his earnestness. "Of course."

She led him into the kitchen where she uncovered the coffee grinder and measured the beans into the top.

"You don't have to go to all that trouble. Instant's fine."

Sure, lots of people liked that disgusting stuff, so she really shouldn't pass judgment on him for his indiscriminating taste. "It's no trouble."

"Nice place here." Bill fingered the rack of neatly organized kitchen utensils, then lifted the cover of a blender to peek underneath. "Lots of gadgets."

Jillian smiled. "They're my toys. I buy kitchen gadgets the way computer hackers buy gizmos and software." The coffee done, Jillian poured a cup of the steaming liquid for Bill. "Sugar or black?"

"Sugar."

Something about the way he said the words made her turn to face him. If she hadn't known better, she would have sworn he'd said it as an affectionate nickname. The heavy-lidded expression that crossed his face was brief, but definite. It was almost immediately replaced by an innocent, questioning stare.

She presented her back to him while she finished with the coffee. Surely she must have been imagining things. Didn't most divorced women miss intimacy after a while? Maybe that's all it was—a hormone attack.

"One spoon of sugar, or two?" she asked, trying to keep the strange uneasiness from her voice. It wouldn't do to stammer and stutter while asking for another chance with her cooking show.

"Three."

She should have known. In some ways, he reminded her of an overgrown boy. In others...well, she thought it best not to dwell on the subject.

Jillian was about to ask him into the living room when he took a seat at the kitchen table. It was a little thing, but it felt too close, too intimate, for comfort. She sat across from him and saw him as he might look in a bathrobe, sipping his morning coffee behind a newspaper.

She *must* stop thinking like this.

"How did you know where to find me tonight?" she asked.

Bill set down his cup and smiled. "A little girl about so high—" he leveled his hand about three feet from the floor "—said you had 'gone exercising.'"

Jillian nodded. "Must have been Alisa, the little girl who lives across the hall. I suppose I should say something to her mother about her talking to strangers."

"And, boy, did she talk." Even though he relaxed back in the straight chrome chair, there was no hint of slouching in his posture. Bill caught her eyes with his and held them. "She told me she has a Barbie doll that looks just like you."

Yes, she would definitely talk to Alisa's mother.

Bill rubbed the pulse point in front of his left ear. Jillian's stomach tightened when his expression turned serious.

He took a sip of his coffee, then leaned forward, propping one elbow on the glass-topped table. "Your six weeks are almost up."

"It's only been four weeks."

"I can't afford to keep losing advertising dollars."

"Are you going back on our agreement?"

Bill groaned.

Jillian would not make it easy for him to just brush her away. "I left a steady job to host this program." She didn't bother to mention that it had been as chief cook at a less-than-five-star restaurant and the only reason she'd worked there was for the money, meager as it was. "I'm fulfilling my job requirements. I haven't missed any time from work, and I've made some creative changes in the program."

"Unfortunately they're not creative enough."

He was right. The changes she'd made had been minor, even superficial. She could alter everything about the show and still be left with one glaring problem: herself. Stage presence, unfortunately, was important to television viewers.

She knew that in order to keep the show she would have to compromise, no matter how much she disliked the idea. Rather than seeing it as a failure on her part, maybe she should take a philosophical approach. Most successful people, in any career, had mentors who helped them get established.

Yes, she would ask Bill Clayton to be her mentor. As her father would say, "A good soldier may have to surrender, but he will do so with a strategy in mind."

"We can work it out," Jillian said at length, "if you're willing to consider my strategy."

"It'll take more than repainting the set."

"I have a plan."

He raised an eyebrow.

Skeptic, she thought. Jillian drew the line at groveling, but she would definitely give it her best try.

"As you know, the show featuring you as my assistant was aired about a month ago."

"And?"

"Well, regardless of whose fault it was, it strangely enough turned out to be a hit with the viewers." It was enough to make her ponder the decline of society. "We got more phone calls and letters after that show than in the entire time I was on my own."

"Yeah, women are still coming up to me in the grocery store and asking for my autograph."

She wasn't sure if it was a complaint, or whether he actually enjoyed the attention.

"I have this sick feeling I know what your point is," Bill said, "but why don't you spell it out for me?"

"You'll let me stay and continue doing the show... and you'll be my assistant." There, she'd said it.

He was shaking his head as soon as the words were out of her mouth. "The only reason I came on the set that day was to lighten the tension. You were so upset about not having an assistant that I thought it would help you relax a little. I was only goofing around. Besides," he added, "I have my own job to do, and I don't know anything about cooking."

"Mr. Reason said the new station manager is taking a big load off your shoulders."

"Mr. Reason has a big mouth." His words weren't angry. He seemed to be merely stating a fact.

"And you don't have to know anything about cooking—that's what I'm there for. You don't even have to prepare for the show. All you need to do is provide the, uh... entertainment factor."

Bill got up and took his empty cup to the sink. With the water running, he mumbled, "I don't know. It probably won't work."

She followed him to the sink. He automatically took her cup and rinsed it as well. "If you help me, we could raise the station's ratings *and* establish my reputation as a culinary professional." Jillian hoped that was the only reputation she established as a result of pairing up with "Boondock Bill."

Bill leaned against the sink, idly swishing water in a cup.

"If it makes you feel any better," Jillian consoled, "I don't relish the idea any more than you do." She had already swallowed her pride to propose such a venture; she refused to beg him.

"You've got two weeks left on our agreement," he acceded. "I suppose we could try it for that long."

"Good, then we'll start tomorrow. Taping begins at ten."

"In that case, I'd better go home and get my beauty sleep," Bill joked.

Jillian followed him to the door. "Bill."

He stopped, his hand on the knob.

"Thanks for giving my show another chance."

"For two more weeks," he amended. He lifted his hand to touch an errant strand of her still-damp hair. "Who knows, it might work out after all."

She got the feeling he wasn't referring to her show. "There's one other thing."

While he waited expectantly, Jillian felt the heat rise to her face. She'd put it off too long already, so she may as well get it over with.

"I'm sorry I called you Boondock Bill."

"In that case," Bill said, amusement dimpling the corner of his mouth, "I'm sorry I called you the most beautiful disaster I've ever seen."

Chapter Three

Some nerve, Jillian thought, for him to call her a disaster. What had ever made her think such a bizarre idea could possibly work?

For the past three days, from the time Bill had stepped in front of the cameras, he had acted like a man possessed. *Ham* was too mild a word to use for him.

He'd started out by interrupting her usual introduction at the opening of the show. Blurting out like some rebel rube, he'd called it "Cookin' With Jill and Boondock Bill" in that overdone accent of his. An argument—which she hoped would end upon the cutting room floor—ensued between them. She hated that he could reduce her to such pitiable behavior.

Another time, when she was explaining the proper procedure for stuffing a game hen, she'd been so perturbed by his tomfoolery that she forgot what came next. Bill had filled the momentary silence by reading a cue card left over from a public-service announcement about preventing teen pregnancy.

She supposed she should have been thankful for the comic distraction. The only time she'd stammered in three days was in the middle of their argument, when she was at a loss for an appropriate name to call him.

Jillian glanced at the wall clock in her office. Almost an hour past her usual departure time. She set about tidying her desk and gathering up her briefcase.

The problem with having Bill on the show, to name but one, was the increased cleanup time. He invariably wound up making characters out of dough, as he'd done today, or mixing food coloring to create the "hottest new fashion shade."

Of its own accord, her mouth turned into an upward curve. She had to admit, it had been funny when he spoofed an old late-night television segment with a flour-dough person and flattened it with a rolling pin.

At the time, it had been all she could do to keep from laughing out loud at his antics. But someone had to keep the show on track.

A telephone call halted her exit. Jillian's exasperation at the intrusion vanished as she remembered this was the reason she had asked Bill Clayton to assist her on the show. The phone had barely stopped ringing since their show aired yesterday afternoon.

This caller wanted Bill's recipe for corn pudding. Jillian took a number and promised to get back to her.

She turned to find Bill's brawny body filling her doorway.

"You're mad at me," he stated.

"No, I'm not." Her answer was too quick, too intense.

"Yes, you are."

He was right. She may as well level with him. "You have been going a bit overboard these past few days."

"Let me make it up to you."

He stepped into her office, filling the room with more than just his body. His clean, albeit doughy, smell. His intensity. His joie de vivre. The space closed between them. Now, like most other times, Jillian felt overwhelmed by him.

His voice was soft, almost like a caress. "Let me take you out for a bite to eat and a little entertainment. It's Friday, and you certainly deserve a break after what I put you through this week."

It was tempting. Heaven knew, she didn't have much of a social life, having lived in the Richmond area less than two months. But something warned her about seeing her employer after working hours. However, she really did need to discuss the show with him. Perhaps if they went to a quiet restaurant, they could talk without interruption.

"Let's just have dinner. We need to get some things straight about the show." She picked up her purse.

"I thought you'd say yes, so I made reservations. If we leave now, we can make it on time." He took her briefcase and tucked her hand in the crook of his elbow. "I hope you like pizza."

It was impossible to talk over the din. The place was heavy on atmosphere, but not the kind Jillian had expected. Nearby, a group of Friday-night revelers, dressed in orange shirts with green lettering, whooped with delight and whacked each other on the back.

Jillian leaned toward Bill. "What did you say?" she yelled across the Formica-topped table.

"I said it seems such a waste to be here and not sling even one ball down the alley."

Jillian took one last bite and laid her pizza crust on the paper plate. It wasn't bad for bowling-alley cuisine.

Over the static of a loud speaker, a garbled voice called Mr. Clayton to lane number four.

"If we don't go now, they'll give our lane reservation to someone else," Bill urged.

Jillian hadn't bowled since summer camp, when she was nine years old. Pins clattered, and the group in orange cheered again. She was already here. What harm could one game do?

"Okay," she said, "but I'm not very good."

"That's never kept me from having a good time."

Jillian had never heard a truer statement. Bill paid for the lane and they put on rented shoes. Although he turned everything he did into a playtime activity, his zeal equaled that of an Olympic contender.

Tonight was no exception.

His exuberance attracted the attention of the team in orange. They'd bowled no more than two frames when members of the Lakeland team began hitching thumbs in their direction and talking among themselves.

"Is that—"

"I don't know. Can't be sure."

Jillian felt her face grow warm. She realized that such recognition came with being a television personality. Nevertheless, their stares and quiet comments unnerved her. How could she get stage fright at a bowling alley?

Trying to ignore her newfound audience, she picked up her ball and approached the lane. Holding the ball in front of her nose as she'd seen others do, Jillian let her arm swing back in a graceful arc and flung it...behind her.

Horrified, she turned around to face the ridicule and snickers that were sure to come.

To her amazement, no one seemed to have noticed. Seated on the bench separating them from the orange team, Bill wrote something on a score pad. The five women in orange clustered over his shoulder, trying to see what he had scribbled.

One woman looked up and, noticing Jillian, pointed to the ball at her feet. "Did you lose that?"

A fellow Lakelander nudged the woman. "Hey, Boondock Bill *and* Jill are here. May as well get her autograph, too."

Feeling like last week's leftovers, Jillian obliged their halfhearted request. Rather than stay and listen to them coo over Bill as they asked him to "talk like a hick," Jillian picked up the big, gold-speckled ball and heaved it down the alley. A gutter ball.

Bill excused himself from the orange-clad entourage. Standing behind her as she wrote her score, he murmured, "The ball's too big for you."

"No, it's not," she argued. "Do you know how many pounds I bench-press on an average day?"

Bill shrugged. He knew what was wrong with her— she was mad because those Lakelanders had made a big deal over him and practically ignored her. It looked like his plan to make things up to her wasn't working. "Suit yourself," he said.

He took his turn and came one pin short of a spare. Much better than usual.

Jillian, on the other hand, almost lost the ball on her downswing. She turned and glared at him, her ice-blue eyes flashing a clear warning to keep his mouth shut.

He had never been good at taking orders.

"The finger holes are too big, Jill. Why don't you try this one with the pink swirls?"

Without a word, she put the ball down and picked up the one he suggested.

He took his turn, knocking down eight pins this time. Bowing and making a sweeping motion with his arm, he cleared the floor for her.

Standing at the ready, she composed herself and lined up the ball with the pins. Her form was great.

Indeed, he'd never seen a better form. She hadn't changed from the prim, no-nonsense dress she'd worn on the show. Her shapely calves stretching with each movement, she released the ball with a powerful throw and stood frozen, waiting for the hit. *Put a toga on her,* Bill thought, *and she'd easily outclass any ancient goddess.*

The pins clattered and fell. All ten of them.

She turned and speared him with a look of smug satisfaction. "My name's Jillian," she said, brushing past him. "Jill's the girl who came tumbling after."

As the game progressed and Jillian's skill improved, her score approached his own. He was less surprised by her competence than by the way she played. With tight-lipped concentration, she'd given it her all, demanding no less than one hundred percent from herself. He hadn't been prepared for such competitiveness from someone who otherwise seemed so mild and restrained.

"You're a real go-getter," he said as they got into the car. The early-October chill prompted him to turn the car's heater on. Looking at the dark-haired beauty beside him, he could think of better ways to warm the car.

"No less than you." Jillian tucked her purse beside her on the seat. "Our styles are just different."

Bill couldn't agree more. "I wasn't sure you liked pizza," he said, hoping to prolong the time to take her home.

Jillian smiled at his remark. Lots of people thought she would eat nothing less than gourmet cooking. "I love junk food. That's why I work out."

"What else do you do in your spare time?"

She shot him a questioning glance, wondering why he was taking this sudden interest in her activities. "TV, weight lifting, public-speaking class. And sometimes I go to Saint Dominick's Church and help cook for the homeless."

He nodded, apparently digesting that last bit of information. "Ever play Nintendo?"

"I've heard of it."

"We could go back to my place, and I'll show you how."

He reminded her of a kindergartner inviting his playmate to join in and play with a new toy. Only trouble was, no kindergartner she ever saw filled out a shirt the way Bill Clayton did.

Hesitating, she asked, "Is that some sort of a line?"

"Would you rather I asked you up to see my etchings?"

"We still haven't talked about the show."

"Okay, we'll talk. Then we'll play Nintendo."

The first thing Jillian noticed when she walked into his apartment was the underwear hanging from the deer antlers. At second glance, she saw socks on the gun-cabinet doorknob, sheets draped over what appeared to be a coat rack, and a shirt hanging from the window latch.

"Oops, forgot I did whites this morning," said Bill as he started gathering up the laundry. "You know what they say—home is where you hang your underwear."

Jillian marveled at how easily he handled an awkward situation with a twisted cliché. She would have been speechless in the same situation, but she had no doubt he would have been just as casual about the predicament if he'd had a television camera aimed at him.

"Doesn't your laundry room have a dryer?" She retrieved a pair of briefs that had fallen to the floor. Size 34. She hastily handed them to him, appalled by her curiosity about his intimate apparel.

"Don't have a laundry room. You're supposed to supply your own washer and dryer. Only trouble is, I don't have a dryer and there's no room for a clothesline out back."

He went to the bedroom and came back empty-handed. He plopped down beside her on the over-stuffed couch. Moving aside a newspaper, *TV Guide*, remote control, and a kernel of popcorn, he propped his shoeless feet on the coffee table. "So what did you want to talk about?"

How could she tactfully tell him he was stealing the show? That episode with the Lakelanders proved as much. She'd go for the direct approach.

"You're stealing the show."

His smile disappeared. "I thought you wanted me to provide the entertainment."

"I do, but I don't want you to keep...taking over." She wished she had insisted on discussing this at the office. With his knee touching hers, she felt much too close. Too vulnerable. "We both need to remember that the show is about cooking, not about Boondock Bill."

Other men would have been insulted. Judging by Bill's reaction, he obviously had the confidence to take it in stride.

"In other words, you want me to leave the 'cutting up' to you?" He seemed pleased by the humor in his statement and started grinning.

Jillian smiled at him, more because of his reaction than because of his corny joke. "No, you should continue to be yourself. But maybe you could ditch the accent."

"All of it?"

"As much as you can."

"Deal. If this staff meeting is adjourned, then I'm going to whup you at Nintendo."

After he'd talked her into staying and playing a few sets of Mario, Jillian had caught on very quickly. So quickly, in fact, that she'd won almost half of their games. He'd easily won the last few, but he suspected she was beginning to tire.

Unable to suppress a dainty yawn, she tried to hide it behind her hand. Bill racked his brain for a reason to delay taking her home. Too bad a sudden, unseasonable blizzard couldn't snow them in for a week.

It was probably just as well. He had no business taking an interest in someone like Jillian. Anyway, she was a little too uptight to suit him.

Except for tonight. Tonight had been different. Kneeling in front of the Nintendo controls with her skirt splayed around her, she seemed very different from the shy, awkward young woman at the station who tried so hard to appear professional and in control.

From the first day he'd seen her he noticed her extraordinary beauty. A man would have to be blind not to. He'd tried to dismiss her beauty as skin-deep, but tonight proved otherwise. She was warm and animated, vibrant and energetic. That combination played havoc with his libido.

Bill had never been more aware of his maleness than when they'd sat side by side, pitted together in competition. Perhaps that was why he'd lost a few games. He'd been concentrating more on the heady fragrance of her perfume and the contrast of dark hair against fair skin than on maneuvering Mario over the obstacles.

Bill gave her a hand up. Her hand seemed small and soft in his. Annoyed with himself, he abruptly retrieved her black wool coat.

Later, at her apartment door, he stood watching Jillian's carefully guarded expression. He wondered if her face would crack if she tried to smile—really smile. Not that well-controlled pose that she usually offered.

Bill never could resist a challenge. He'd make her smile.

For now, he'd settle for just shaking her composure a little.

Jillian had just unlocked the door and was turning to say something when he stepped closer and pulled her body to his. They went together like summer showers and rainbows.

Bill kissed her, half expecting her to pull back or say something that would effectively put him in his place. She did neither. Instead she returned his kiss, tentatively at first, then bolder as their passions unleashed.

The sound of their breathing seemed to fill the tiny hallway that separated Jillian's apartment from her neighbor's. Suddenly aware of how close the next unit was, Bill reluctantly ended the kiss. He wondered if he'd ever get used to the fact that people around here lived like cattle in a boxcar.

His mouth still warm from the heat of their kiss, Bill rubbed a thumb over the whisker burn at the corner of her lips. No smile yet, but she did look a bit dazed.

"I'd better let you go inside before your neighbors get curious."

Jillian nodded. The pale blue of her eyes seemed less penetrating and more liquid in the aftermath of their kiss.

Seeking to lighten the thick tension that hung between them, Bill changed the subject.

"What I want to know," Bill said, running the pad of his finger along her delicately curved jawline, "is whether you really lost that last game of Nintendo or if you were just sucking up to the boss."

Immediately he regretted his words. The light in her eyes glittered with ice as she abruptly pulled away.

Jillian drew back and pushed the door open. How could she have been so stupid? She had no business kissing Bill. He was her employer and co-worker. Although she usually objected to his outspokenness, tonight she was thankful he'd broken the spell of craziness that had besieged her.

What she wasn't thankful for, however, was the implication that she would use a game—or anything else— to secure favors from Bill.

"It appears that I've given you the wrong impression," she said, her voice as polished as she could manage under the circumstance. "I assure you I had no such intentions."

"Jillian, I didn't mean—"

"As for what took place just now . . . it won't happen again. Good night."

Jillian stepped inside and closed the door. Leaning against the wooden barricade, she felt her knees weaken. Why did that man have such an effect on her?

He'd done nothing to indicate he wanted to take their relationship to a personal level. If he'd taken her to an elegant restaurant and dancing afterward, she would have suspected he was interested in something other than a night out with a friend followed by a discussion about work. One could hardly classify bowling and Nintendo as an attempt at romantic involvement.

His behavior had been respectful and polite. As for the goodnight kiss, perhaps he'd meant it as merely that—a goodnight kiss. Then, when she had responded so eagerly, he had naturally followed through. And why wouldn't he? He was a man.

An unpredictable, amusing, countrified man with a body that wouldn't quit.

With a sinking feeling, Jillian knew she'd have a tough time keeping her promise.

That episode Friday night had somehow, inexplicably, changed things between Jillian and Bill.

Over the next few days, she found herself striving to keep things impersonal between them. Unfortunately, no matter how hard she tried, she couldn't help laughing at his antics and feeding him lines that he would be certain to turn into a joke or a visual gag. She tried to attribute the well of pleasure that bubbled whenever he was around to the lack of his cornball accent and the fact that her show was becoming a local hit.

He was fun. Jillian's upbringing had neglected that part of her education.

And if Bill seemed a little more intimate, touching her as he passed the ingredients and making jokes about bowling...well, it was probably only a result of learning the give-and-take necessary for a successful cohost relationship.

By the end of Jillian's six-week probation period, the show was attracting attention around Richmond, not only for Jillian, but for the station as well. The advertising slots for her shows were usually almost filled, and advertising was quickly picking up during other times as well.

"Looks like you got yourself a permanent show," Bill said as he tied on his Kiss the Cook apron. "Memphis took a few demo tapes back home, and he's going to try to get the local station to run the show. We've got a couple of other leads for the Tidewater and Fredericksburg areas."

Bill grinned at Jillian, and she felt her heart turn somersaults. She wasn't sure whether it was due to the news or the messenger.

"Keep up the good work, my lady, and we may even get syndicated."

"Syndicated?" Maybe her dream *would* come true before she reached thirty.

"Not to the Big Three. Not just yet, anyway. But if my hunch is correct, 'Cooking With Jillian' should go over big in rural communities." He lifted a lid and sniffed. "After we're established with the independent stations, we'll go for the big guys."

Jillian had difficulty controlling her excitement during the taping of their show. It looked like she and Bill would be teamed up for quite a while.

A month ago she would have been horrified by that prospect. Now, with him standing beside her, grating cheese as deftly as he wisecracked, she found herself looking forward to a morning of taping, rather than dreading it as she had before.

After they finished topping the casserole with cheese, Jillian picked up the dish to put it in the oven.

Bill stepped forward and reached for it. "Allow me."

"No, that's okay. I've got it."

But she didn't. As the ovenware started to slip from Jillian's grasp, Bill stepped around and caught it by one handle. With an awkward half step and a twirl, he wound up sprawled over the counter, one hand around the dish and the other gripping Jillian's arm.

Jillian was undecided as to whether it had been a fall or a pratfall. She debated whether to comfort him or say something funny. He beat her to it.

"How about that?" Bill said, playing to the camera. "A dish in each hand. Don't know which is more delectable."

Jillian tried to step out of his reach, but found herself tangled in his microphone cord. She sighed, wondering if this latest travesty would end up on the air along with all the others. Remembering her initial fear that her reputation as an accredited chef would be tarnished by the shenanigans that pervaded the set, Jillian made a slicing motion across her throat.

"Cut this from the final version, will you, Darlene?"

"And while you're at it," Bill added, "order one of those mikes that hangs from the ceiling."

Jillian stepped closer to Bill, letting the line go slack so they could unwind the mess. She tried not to notice their closeness or that his nearness caused her to tremble.

"On second thought," Bill said, smiling down at her, "Cancel that order."

Jillian blushed as his eyes raked over her. Trying to avoid his green-gray gaze, she busied herself in an attempt to untie their microphones. Her fingers shook.

Seemingly undaunted, Bill brushed the tip of her nose. "Flour. You have it on your clothes, too." His voice was husky, as if his mind was on something besides her flour-dusted face.

"Somebody, throw a bucket of water on them," Darlene shouted.

"Maybe we should just take them off," Jillian suggested.

With a devilish lift of one eyebrow, Bill cast her a glance that could be mistaken for nothing other than desire.

"The microphones," she amended, although thinking about his interpretation gave her warm feelings in places that ached for his touch. Self-consciously she added, "Maybe we should take the microphones off and then try to untangle them."

"Oh." He sounded disappointed. Oddly enough, he sounded the way Jillian felt.

"What do you want me to do about it?" Bill leaned back in his chair and propped his running shoes on his desk.

What did she want him to do about it? Was he that obtuse? "I want you to stop overruling me. I specifically asked Darlene to cut that microphone fiasco from the final version. Not to mention your crack about serving mountain oysters as hors d'oeuvres, or the incident involving that rubber chicken."

"I agree we got carried away those days."

Jillian drew herself up and raised an eyebrow, trying to maintain a serious expression despite remembering the rubber-chicken episode.

"Okay, *I* got carried away, but I didn't overrule you." He chuckled and laced his fingers behind his head. "You have to admit they were pretty funny. And the microphone thing was really popular with the viewers. We're still getting calls on that."

"Darlene said she was told to leave them in." The statement was more a question than an accusation. He might be an infuriating prankster, but he certainly wasn't a liar. "If you didn't tell her, who did?"

The door swung open, almost hitting the arm of Jillian's chair. "Hey there, buddy, guess what?" Memphis stopped when he noticed Jillian sitting across the desk from his friend. "Sorry, didn't realize you had company." He gave Bill an obvious wink and started to leave.

"Come in and have a seat," Bill said as he rose to pull up a spare chair. Turning to Jillian, he said, "Looks like we found the answer to your question."

Instead of sitting, Memphis put a big cowboy boot on the chair and leaned an elbow on his knee. Jillian got the impression the man didn't sit much. Except maybe in his truck.

"Listen here, buddy—you too, Jill, since this involves you—I took them demo tapes down to that station you told me about and they want to use your show! Their place is almost as rinky-dink as this one, but that still ought to do you proud."

The big man grinned and scratched his bearded cheek as they bombarded him with questions.

"Heck, that ain't the half of it. I just called them folks in Fredericksburg and Norfolk, and both of them are gonna give you a try. Three for three. You can't beat that with a stick.''

Bill stuck out his hand. ''Memph, I was all set to ream you out about your meddling ways, but let's just call it even.''

They shook hands while Jillian looked on in shocked silence. Three stations would be airing her show. ''Cooking With Jillian'' might soon be syndicated.

Although she wasn't superstitious, she knocked the wood on the arm of her chair to prevent bad luck. She was so close. She mustn't let anything go wrong now.

Chapter Four

The first negative letter arrived a week after the show started airing outside the Richmond area.

The message was clear: The writer didn't like the show and wanted her off the air. The letter rambled on and even threatened to "take care of her" this weekend. There was no signature.

Unbidden, the thought of movie and television actors being stalked by demented fans wormed its way into her mind. What if this was truly the work of a dangerous person?

Jillian slowly shook her head. What if she was just overreacting to a crank letter? It was probably from some flaky person with nothing better to do than bother innocent people. Nevertheless it unsettled her. Fortunately her address was not included in the local phone directory.

She refolded the terse typewritten note and tucked it next to her telephone where it would serve as a reminder that it's impossible to please everyone.

By Saturday, when she was helping serve meals at Saint Dominick's, she had almost forgotten the incident.

Scooping a dipper full of the chili she'd helped make this morning, she thought with satisfaction of the hungry stomachs it would fill. Topping the thick concoction with grated cheese, she handed the bowl to a thin, elderly man in baggy jeans and a light jacket.

"Whatzis junk? I was hoping we were gonna get fish sticks today. Fish sticks are better than anything else they serve around here."

Jillian was too stunned to respond. Perhaps she'd been too quick to pat herself on the back.

Lydia relieved her discomfort when she plopped a square of corn bread—made with Jillian's favorite recipe—on the man's tray. "You don't know what a treat you're in for. Miss Reed is a chef, and she helped us make this chili."

"I useta be a chef, too, and I always put garvon spice in my chili." He lifted the tray and sniffed. "Humph! Don't smell no garvon spice in here." He walked to the row of folding tables, muttering as he went.

Jillian's heart went out to the man. Seeing a former chef come through this lunch line made his situation uncomfortably close for Jillian. "What's his name?" she asked Lydia. "I'd like to talk to him."

"Why?"

It was a good question. One for which Jillian wasn't sure she had the answer. "I want to ask him where I can find garvon spice."

Lydia and a middle-aged man in line started laughing. At Jillian's confusion, Lydia said, "There's no such thing as garvon spice. He made it up, just like he made up that story about being a chef."

The man in line picked up a napkin and spoon. "Last month Cooter was the doctor who had discovered the cure for Guggenheim's disease. And the month before that, he was the inventor of the water bed. He's a little . . . you know." He circled a finger around his ear.

Jillian tried not to think about the unfortunate old man as she finished dishing out bowls full of chili. The past several times she had come to help, she had stayed in the kitchen. Today her eyes had been opened.

"That looks like the last one," said Lydia. "Now the fun part begins. Do you want to wash or dry?"

"You choose." On her way to the kitchen, Jillian noticed Cooter gathering up trays left on the tables.

As they worked over the hot sink, Lydia asked, "It was different from what you expected, wasn't it?"

Jillian shut her eyes, wishing once again there was something more she could do. "I expected the old clothes and some of the crudeness that I saw. It was the women, families, and young, healthy-looking men that surprised me. And that man who was telling us about the places he'd visited before his wife died and he started drinking. . . ." She handed Lydia the clean chili pot. "It's so sad to think that the next time they come, they'll be just as hungry and just as down on their luck as they are today."

"Don't let it discourage you. Most of the families are from the housing project. Just remember that it's a meal they might not otherwise get. Helping them through one more day is a bigger accomplishment than you might imagine."

The door pushed open, and Cooter walked in. Rummaging through the pantry closet, he muttered something to himself. Then he left, clutching a broom and dustpan.

When he came back to put the cleaning items away, he picked up the foil-wrapped corn bread Lydia had left on the counter. As he tucked the package under his thin coat, he shot Lydia a snaggle-toothed grin.

Lydia smiled back at him as he left. "See you next time, Cooter." She turned to Jillian and explained, "He has a nervous condition. If he doesn't stay busy, he gets real irritable. We can't pay him for helping, but he's happy with the take-out service."

"You can't park there, miss." The uniformed officer motioned her toward a parking area farther away from her apartment building.

Preoccupied with her thoughts about the people she'd met in the food line today, Jillian only now noticed the yellow police tape roping off a wide berth around her unit. Some of her neighbors clustered beyond the flashing lights of police and fire vehicles. She spotted Mr. Henderson, her downstairs neighbor who worked nights, wearing corduroy slippers and a plaid flannel robe.

Hastily parking her car, Jillian got out and ran toward the frightened group. Her heart in her throat, she saw little Alisa and her mother.

"Fay, is there a fire? What's going on?"

"A bad person did it," Alisa piped in. "The polices are gonna put him in jail."

"Arson? Somebody set our building on fire?"

"Well, not exactly . . ." Fay began.

Then Jillian saw him, talking animatedly with a policeman, his arms gesturing wildly. With a sickening jolt, she realized they were questioning Bill Clayton.

What was he doing here? Had he seen something—or someone?

Then she remembered the threatening note she'd received recently. The writer had promised to "take care of her" this weekend. Fear twisted in the pit of her stomach. Her apartment was in jeopardy, and here was Bill, right in the thick of things. She dreaded to think that he might have come face-to-face with the perpetrator.

"Apparently there was a bomb threat," Fay said, her voice lowered so as not to alarm Alisa. "About twenty minutes ago, someone found a cardboard box at your door. A string was connected from the box to your doorknob. Mr. Henderson said whoever did it probably thought you were inside. Then, when you would have opened the door to come out, the string would detonate the device."

"Oh, my." Jillian's hand automatically went to her mouth to quell the nausea that rose in her throat. Why would someone do this to her? What had she done to cause anyone to be so vengeful?

Fay gripped Jillian's arm. "Are you all right? Maybe you should sit down."

Jillian started to follow her friend to the car. A wave of paranoia hit, and Jillian suddenly felt as though she were wearing a bull's-eye on her chest. What if the person who had tried to kill her was still lurking about, waiting for a second chance? When Alisa reached up and curled her tiny fingers around Jillian's hand, she fought an indefinable urge to run.

Suddenly she wanted to be near the police and the protection of their guns. Near Bill's familiar presence. And she wanted to get away from her neighbors, who had been unwittingly caught up in a grudge involving Jillian.

"Thanks," Jillian muttered, pulling free of the mother and daughter, "but I'd better go talk to them."

Numbly she made her way toward the blue flashing lights. Her feet were moving, but it was as though they were detached from her body. All feelings seemed to have left her, and Jillian was glad. For, along with her other sensations, the intense panic that had seized her a moment ago was now dulled as well. The squawking of the emergency radios and excited chatter around her seemed to dim, and Jillian couldn't feel her feet touch the ground.

Bill looked up, relief washing over him as he saw Jillian approach. Her eyes fixed straight ahead, her usually translucent skin suddenly went chalky.

Bill lurched forward, catching her in his arms as she started to stumble. Lieutenant Greer opened the back door of the police cruiser, and Bill maneuvered her inside.

Once settled, he couldn't seem to let go. Holding her tightly against him, he rested his cheek against her shiny dark hair and fought back the emotions that welled within him. First, there'd been the overpowering fear, when he'd been unable to find her, that she'd been hurt. Relief at seeing her was quickly replaced by the need to protect her from the ugly situation she was now caught up in.

Stroking the hair away from her clammy face, he kissed her lightly on the temple. "Don't you worry about anything now, honey. I'm going to take care of you." He pressed her head to his chest and started circling the flat of his hand over her back, as a parent might soothe a small child.

His warmth encircled Jillian. She melted into the safety net that he had spread around her, wrapping her arms tightly around his strong torso. His calm strength eased the shallow-breathing panic she'd experienced a moment before, and she sought to get closer to the source of that strength. She drew from it, allowing it to surge through her body, filling her with a sense of calm security. Jillian wanted to stay like this, forever in the comfort of Bill's arms.

The front door opened, and a police officer got in. "Is she okay?"

Bill nodded, and Jillian felt the roughness of his chin as it chafed her forehead. "Just a mite woozy for a second or two. Shock, I guess."

As the blood flowed back to her brain, Jillian realized how she must look to them. A weak female reacting to the trauma of learning she could have been killed. Reluctantly she pulled away from the comfort of Bill's embrace. Although he didn't resist as she drew away, his left arm remained draped across her shoulders.

In an effort to restore her dignity, Jillian straightened her posture, adjusted the tumble of dark hair on her shoulders, and smoothed her skirt. But she didn't ask Bill to move his arm. Didn't want him to.

"Why didn't you tell me you'd gotten threatening letters?" Bill's voice was gentle, but insistent.

"It was just one. I thought it was from someone with a weird sense of humor."

The police officer made a note on his clipboard. "There's nothing funny about it, Miss Reed. Whoever did this means business."

Bill explained that the weekend receptionist had seen the letter on her desk while leaving a phone message, and brought it to his attention. Alarmed, Bill had immediately come to check on her and found the suspicious box tied to her doorknob. That was when he had called the police. When she didn't answer the phone and no one seemed to know where she might be, he panicked.

"Thank God you're all right," he said, squeezing her shoulder.

Jillian gave him a weak smile. There was no mistaking the concern in his eyes.

Jillian answered some questions for Lieutenant Greer. Impatient with the situation and the unfairness of it, Jillian wished it was all behind her. She'd done nothing to deserve this.

The lieutenant handed her a card. "Call this number if you get any more threats or if you see anything suspicious."

Two men in protective gear emerged from the building, casually carrying a brown box between them. As they approached the squad car, Jillian could see they were smiling.

Just then, Alisa broke free from her mother's grasp, ran toward the men and jerked the box away from them. Jillian and Bill stepped out of the squad car but still couldn't hear their exchange. It was obvious Alisa was angry. It was also just as obvious that the bomb experts were quite amused by her.

"She's really giving them what-for," Bill said with a chuckle.

Alisa spun around and stalked toward Jillian, the large box banging against the girl's knees.

Jillian knelt down as her little neighbor approached. Tears replaced the anger of a moment ago, and drops rolled down Alisa's cheeks. The sight tore at Jillian's heart.

"They messed up my surprise."

Jillian hugged her. "They didn't mean to, sweetie."

One of the men from the bomb crew stepped forward, still grinning. "Show her what's in the box, Alisa."

Pulling the cardboard flaps open, she said, "I cooked a pie for you. Now it's all messed up."

"Oh, Alisa, that was so sweet." Jillian reached into the box and withdrew an aluminum pie plate filled with sunbaked mud adorned by pebbles, grass, twigs, and something that looked suspiciously like dead insects. "It's not ruined," she assured the child. "It looks very, um . . . appetizing."

Bill leaned closer. "Those little brown things. They're not—"

"They're *raisins*," Jillian quickly supplied.

"Chocolate chips," Alisa countered.

Jillian tried not to look too closely at the backyard concoction. "Alisa, it was very thoughtful of you to make this pie for me. But why did you put it in that big box and tie it to my doorknob?"

Alisa sighed and dramatically rolled her eyes as if any idiot could have figured it out. "So robbers wouldn't steal it!"

The police confessed the combination of mud pies and bombs was a first for them. The group of people had dispersed after delivering some teasing remarks.

The experience seemed to be a big joke for everyone else, especially after they learned the box's contents.

Jillian, however, was still quite shaken. Reluctant to be alone, she invited Bill in for a cup of cocoa.

"I can see the headlines now," Bill quipped. *"Chef's neighbor bakes pie, recipe bombs."*

Jillian patted the cushion beside her. "Why don't you sit down and relax. Drink some hot chocolate. That always helps calm my nerves."

Bill didn't sit, neither did he step aside for her to go past. Instead he touched her arm, giving it a light stroke. He spoke in a soft voice. "I wish I'd known that half an hour ago. I was afraid you were going to pass out."

The concern in his eyes made her uncomfortable. Maybe it was because he seemed to see beneath the protective shell she tried to wrap herself in. Or maybe it was because the seriousness he now wore was so different from the endearing comic bumpkin he portrayed on television. Although she was learning to deal with Boondock Bill's antics, she had no idea how to cope with this other side of Bill Clayton.

"I'm sorry I acted like such a wimp—"

"You're safe now. That's all that matters." He took both of her hands in his. "Just promise that you'll let me know if you get any more threatening letters."

"Bill, it was just some crackpot who didn't have anything better to do."

He gave a half smile, but his eyes remained serious. "Do I have to pull rank?"

He was still holding her hands. Jillian wanted to break free—of more than his touch. Of this crazy spell he seemed to have cast over her. She had heard of crime victims becoming emotionally attached to their rescuers. She supposed it was possible for the same to happen to her. Even though it hadn't been an actual crime, emotions had run high and she had welcomed Bill's presence.

She knew he was waiting for an answer. She would give him an appropriately dignified response—let him know that although she had succumbed to the tension of a while ago, she would not fall to pieces over each unkind letter or negative phone call. And by downplaying the incident, she might help ease the concern that was so evident in his eyes.

"I see no need to get worked up over every crank out there who wants to complain."

Bill clamped his lips together until they became a hard line. Releasing her hands, he turned away from Jillian and ran his fingers through the hair above his ear. He took a couple of steps away from her. Jillian thought he was going to start pacing again, but he turned back to face her. From his expression, she expected a lecture about people in the public eye needing to be extra careful.

As quickly as it appeared, the anger drained from his face. When he spoke, it sounded as though his throat had tightened and he was forcing the words out. He tugged at his shirt collar as if to confirm her thought.

"I was worried about you, Jillian."

His eyes met hers and held them, revealing as much in their depths as he stole from her. His weren't the eyes of a television-station owner concerned about the safety of his employee. They were the eyes of a man who wanted to protect his woman, yet felt powerless to do so.

"Oh, Bill."

Then they were in each other's arms. She wasn't sure who made the first move. All she knew was the feel of his long, lean torso pressed hard against her breasts. His arms holding her close. The smell of woodsy after-shave. The firm evidence of his arousal against her abdomen. His breath against her ear, and then his lips against her cheek.

She lifted her face to him, willing away the physical barriers that separated them. His mouth covered hers, sparking in her a fever she had never known before. It felt as though she were drowning in his embrace, and she welcomed the wave of passion that washed over her.

Her fingers slid up to cup his face, a face coarse and rough with dark, afternoon shadow, but oh so touchable.

Her body reveled as his big hands roamed over it, down to the small of her back, the curve of her hips. The gentle reverence of his touch was like that of an antique collector treasuring the delicate symmetry of a beautiful and shapely vase. He made her feel tiny and fragile.

When his lips melded with hers, she knew a sense of rightness she'd never felt before. Her facade of primness stripped away and her soul laid bare to his knowing eyes, Jillian abandoned herself to the power of the man. She gave in to the raw need that surged between them, not caring for the moment that Bill was aware of her need.

The hot crushing pressure of his lips on hers was enough to scatter all threads of logic, all excuses. She gave herself to him, opening herself to this tentative new emotional bond that had grown between them.

His tongue touched her sensitized mouth. Parting her lips, she drew him in.

Jillian heard his sharp, shallow breaths. His hands clamped tighter against her hips, and he pulled her to him. There was no mistaking that he wanted her as badly as she wanted him.

Bill kissed her again, this time with an effort at restraint. Jillian slowly opened her eyes and met the intensity of his gaze. It was obvious he knew how much she wanted him. He seemed pleased and sure of himself at the same time.

As her breathing returned to normal and her brain cleared, she realized they'd somehow crossed the living room and now stood near the short hallway leading to her bedroom. Her lips tingled from the urgency of their kisses.

Had she led him here? Had she led him on? As much as her body wanted to complete what they'd started, Jillian knew she must regain some semblance of control.

Taking a deep, steadying breath, Jillian removed her arms from around Bill's neck and stepped back, away from him and away from the torrent of desire he had unleashed in her.

Bill didn't attempt to restrain her. He just watched her, waiting as if willing her to return to his arms to consummate the heady pleasure they had begun.

Jillian avoided his eyes as she tried to ignore her still-racing heart. The blood throbbed in her neck and ears. She straightened her posture and cleared the huskiness from her throat.

"It seems as though I've overreacted to this afternoon's excitement." It hurt her to know she might be bruising his ego, but it was better that he believed she'd relied on the comfort and security he represented rather than Bill Clayton himself. "I wouldn't want to give you the wrong impression," she added softly.

He saw right through her, and Jillian knew when one corner of his mouth turned slightly upward that he wouldn't go along with the pretense.

"Oh, I doubt I got the wrong impression." Bill lightly ran the knuckle of his forefinger across his reddened mouth. "It was an indelible impression, but I doubt it was the wrong one." He stepped past her and opened the door. "Call me if you need me," he said over his shoulder.

The door closed behind him, then opened again.

"Or even if you just want me."

It seemed Jillian did want Bill.

After the tender moments she had shared with him last Saturday, she spent the first part of the week looking for excuses to be near him.

Of course, she told herself she had legitimate reasons for going to his office or calling him on the phone. The truth was, she could have found the answers to her questions elsewhere.

But the questions she truly wanted answered involved the feelings he had evoked last weekend. And had he experienced those same feelings?

Jillian had even debated with herself whether it was foolish to consider becoming emotionally involved with a man like Bill Clayton. She had almost convinced herself they might get along together off the show as well as they did on it.

Showing up on the set one afternoon, dressed in jacket and tie, neatly pressed slacks, and leather dress shoes, Bill looked like the epitome of a hardworking, respectable businessman. Amazed at the transformation, Jillian had remarked on his appearance during taping.

Bill grinned at the camera, cast her a sidelong glance, and wiggled his eyebrows. "Back home we call this a wooing suit," he said. "Is it working yet?"

Flattered and a little emboldened by his overt flirtation of the past few days, Jillian picked up the young turkey hen she'd been preparing and held it upright in front of Bill. "Must be. She has absolutely lost her head over you."

He appeared pleased by her unexpected witticism. And, for some reason, that pleased Jillian.

Taking another look at her cohost, Jillian noticed with feminine appreciation how well the blazer hugged his broad shoulders and narrowed down to his trim waist. As her grandmother would have said, he certainly cleaned up well.

To make matters more tempting, he had recently stopped the overdrawn accent. Jillian decided she rather liked his natural, soft southern drawl. It brought to mind images of long hikes along hilly, wooded paths and of sipping iced tea while sitting on a porch swing.

Bill had also cut out much of the infuriating silliness from his Boondock Bill character. Now, rather than slapstick, he was charming and funny. His humor more closely complemented Jillian's personality, serving to coax her from her reserved shell rather than stripping it off in front of so many viewers.

Today Jillian was in top form, delivering her own brand of humor and repartee. So she was surprised when Bill touched a hot pan and then let out a series of whoops that made him sound like one of the Three Stooges. Assuming he had dropped back into his old Boondock Bill character, she ad-libbed by picking up the fire extinguisher and pretending an interest in using it on him.

She was aiming the nozzle when she noticed him staring at the red blister forming between his thumb and forefinger.

"Oh my gosh, you're really hurt!" Jillian put down the canister and rushed to the sink to fill a bowl with cold water. Setting it on the counter in front of Bill, she took his injured hand and started to put it into the water when she remembered his jacket. "Why don't you take that off so your sleeve won't get wet?"

"Sure thing," Bill said, a devilish grin sneaking across his face. "Anything else you want me to take off?"

Jillian's cheeks grew warm as she remembered how they'd almost ended up in her bedroom. He'd left her an open invitation that day, and now it seemed as though he wanted to make it clear he was still waiting.

She went to the freezer to put some distance between them while he removed his apron and jacket. After plunking several ice cubes into the water, she immersed Bill's hand. Suddenly aware of his wolfish grin and the crisp curls of brown hair where she held his wrist, she sought to distract herself from his uneasy nearness.

"This is a perfect example of why you should never allow horseplay in the kitchen," Jillian said to the still-rolling camera. Then she chattered on about the importance of treating burns immediately with cold water.

She carefully described each step as she dried the burn with a clean towel and prepared to wrap the area with gauze.

Bill finally spoke up, his voice soft, yet compelling. "Never mind the lecture," he said, stepping closer, "just kiss it and make it better."

For one brief, insane moment, Jillian imagined censors cutting Bill's comment from the show. That voice rightfully belonged in the bedroom scene of at least an R-rated movie. Or was she the only one who noticed the quiet intensity, the unspoken challenge?

"As you know," Jillian said, almost dropping the long strip of gauze as she tried to ignore Bill's penetrating stare, "it's important to keep the area free of germs."

With a sly smile, Bill took the bandage from her fumbling fingers and finished wrapping it himself.

The attraction seemed to hang in the air between them. Jillian smiled at the irony of her interest in him. In a thousand years, she would never have guessed she'd find a man like Bill so compelling, so—

Snapping her attention back to the turkey croquettes, she decided it would be wise to separate whatever personal interest she held in Bill from their professional relationship as cohosts.

No matter how much he made her heart flip with that spontaneous, infectious smile, she must remember her goal. Time was running out, and she didn't want to waste a single opportunity by letting herself get distracted.

She finished shaping the turkey pieces into croquettes. Picking up the pan to pop it into the oven, she was surprised to hear the microwave oven humming.

"What are you doing? We're not preparing anything in the microwave."

"You're not, but I've got somewhere to go tonight. And since we're running late, I thought I'd save some time by cooking supper here." At the sound of the bell, Bill opened the microwave door with his bandaged hand

and extracted a dish with the other. "Zap Burgers. Want one?"

With a sickening jolt, Jillian's heart fell to her stomach. Suddenly the pieces all fell together. The wooing suit. Somewhere to go this evening. Maybe he had a date tonight. Even the flirting fit into the scenario. In an obviously romantic mood, it seemed Bill had let his anticipation spill over to the nearest person available.

An unexpected disappointment filled her as she realized that bedroom voice might not have been meant for her. Had he been thinking of Jillian or someone else when he had flashed her that playful smile and teasingly asked her to kiss the burn on his hand?

Why did it hurt so much?

That Bill might have a date tonight did seem to explain his behavior today. But what about last Saturday at her apartment? He had seduced her and seemed as interested as she in finishing what they'd started.

But that had nothing to do with whether he was going out with someone tonight, Jillian reminded herself. They had no personal commitment between them, and it was best if things stayed that way.

She turned her attention back to the dish she was preparing. She would do better to keep her mind on the business at hand.

"Are you sure you don't want one?" Bill thrust the plate of hamburgers at her. "I could melt some rat cheese on it if you'd like."

She glanced up into the eyes that mirrored her own emotions. Gray for how depressed she felt right now, and green for that twinge of jealousy because she wasn't the one he'd be wooing tonight.

"No thank you." Jillian's movements were purposefully swift and efficient as she busied herself with the croquettes. "Now, if you don't mind giving me a hand over here," she said, hiding behind the businesslike facade, "we have some croquettes to finish."

The next morning, Bill was even more animated than usual. Jillian thought it disgusting the way he went around giving a victory smile and high-fives to everyone he passed. Was he always this blatant about his conquests, she wondered?

When he got to Jillian, where she was preparing the set for the morning's taping, he gave her a giant hug. Lifting her off the floor, he twirled them both a couple of spins, set her down and beamed broadly.

"You got a minute?" he asked. "I want to tell you all about last night. My wooing suit was hotter than it's ever been."

The audacity of this man! She didn't want to hear about the trophy he'd netted—or bedded—last night. Jillian gritted her teeth and started whacking an onion with a knife.

"You'd better be careful. You could hurt yourself with that thing."

Jillian considered turning the blade on him, then quickly remembered it would be harder to achieve the success she sought if she killed the station's owner.

"Look, I'm rather busy right now." She ran out of onion and started chopping a carrot. Her former psychology professor would have a field day with the implications of this action. "Besides, your little tale of conquest is something Memphis would appreciate more than I would. Why don't you share it with him instead?"

Jillian was amazed at how controlled her voice sounded. How could he flirt with one girl while thinking of another?

She shouldn't be so shocked, she supposed. Her ex-husband had made love to her while thinking of his mistress. She wondered if it had something to do with the Y chromosome. If so, she was prepared to give up men altogether.

"Yeah, you're right," Bill was saying. "He'd get a real charge out of it. But I still want you to meet Susan. She's got some great ideas on how to attract more viewers."

Somehow Jillian managed to finish the show without biting her tongue completely off. A couple of times, he asked her if something was wrong, but she changed the subject. She had quickly learned that anything said or done during taping was likely to end up on the air.

Afterward Bill mentioned that he wanted to ask her something.

Oh no, Jillian thought. He was going to keep after her until he got an answer. What could she say? *Oh, Bill, it's just that I was, um, sort of falling in like with you, and I wasn't really expecting a Susan to be in the picture.*

Perhaps she could give him one of her famous icy stares. The look was enough to quell even the most persistent interrogators. No, that worked on everyone but Bill, who somehow always managed to melt the ice to a pile of slush.

He fell in step beside her and walked with her back to her office.

Jillian sat at her desk and motioned for Bill to take the guest chair. With a desk between them, she should feel less off kilter in his presence.

Bill ignored the chair and sat on the edge of her desk.
The exuberance he'd demonstrated earlier was now replaced by a self-satisfied smile.

"I want you to go home with me to meet my parents," he said.

Jillian dropped the paper clip she'd been toying with.
"To Fullerton? To meet your parents?" This was not at
all what she had expected.

"Yep. How about it?"

"You're joking, right?"

Chapter Five

Bill's smile disappeared as he contemplated her reaction. Even though he saw her as a classy woman, one who liked to dress well, eat well, and above all act the part of a sophisticated woman of the world, he'd never taken her for a snob.

"Is there something *wrong* with Fullerton? Or my parents?"

The Lady of Poise faltered. "Oh, no, it's just that... what about Susan?"

"Susan? My media consultant?" Try as he might, Bill wondered if he'd ever figure this woman out. "She'll be here when we get back. We won't be gone for more than a week or two at most."

Jillian sat there, biting the inside of her cheek to keep from smiling at his revelation that his "date" last night had merely been a business meeting. She didn't even try to understand the feeling of relief that flooded her senses.

"Look, maybe I should have given you more background on this before expecting you to go along with it." He stood and leaned against the wall, his legs crossed at the ankles. "My parents own a diner that's something of a trucker's paradise. In fact, that's where I met Memphis. He's originally from Tennessee, but then I suppose you already guessed that."

Jillian sat with erect posture, her hands in her lap, waiting for him to continue.

"Anyway, Susan and I were discussing ways of picking up more viewers, and she suggested that you and I could demonstrate more everyday cooking. Heck, I figured you can't get more everyday than the down-home cooking my mama serves at the diner. You two could spend a week or so learning from each other! What do you think?"

"I'm already committed for the next two Saturdays to cook for the homeless."

She actually seemed glad to have an excuse. Well, he wouldn't let her slip out of going so easily. This change would expand their audience from a cult following to a much broader range of viewers. He was determined to make it work.

"I'll hire someone to take your place."

She considered that for a moment. "Where would we stay?"

"My parents' house. Kylie—my sister—is away at school, so that'll give us an extra room. Don't worry, you'll come home with your reputation intact—my mother and all the citizens of Fullerton will see to that."

"Do you think this scheme will really make a difference?" she asked skeptically.

"Yes. Or I wouldn't ask you to do it."

Bill couldn't claim that as the total truth. He did believe the ploy would work in their favor, and it made a
good excuse for getting her away from the work envi-
ronment. Fullerton was a great place to let your hair
down. He was actually looking forward to dealing with
Jillian on his own turf.

Yes, indeed, she'd have to let her hair down in Fullerton. Folks back home would see to that.

"Too bad it's turning dark already," Bill said. "The
leaves are always spectacular at this time of year."

Jillian glanced at Bill, his hand draped loosely over
the steering wheel. He certainly looked a lot more at
ease than she felt. She must have been half-loco to have
agreed to come with him. Then again, if he had told her
that by closing her eyes, turning around three times and
making a wish her show would be more successful,
she'd have given that a try, too.

However, since she'd be in close quarters with Bill for
as long as two weeks, she'd have to keep her wits and try
to resist his rough-hewn charm.

A car approached on the narrow, winding road,
sending a beam of light directly across Bill's face. The
shadow and light made his deep-set eyes appear even
deeper, his sandy brown hair even darker. She could see
why he was so successful at charming the ladies. In his
own casual way, he was quite handsome. Darlene had
commented on his appeal more than once, going so far
as to say it was too bad he preferred brunettes over
blondes such as herself.

Subconsciously Jillian reached up to wrap a strand of
her own deep brown locks around her finger. She remained lost in thought until a short while later when Bill
turned onto a dirt road.

Bill drove slowly down the washboard surface, allowing Jillian a bumpy view of the neighboring houses. Most were set a good distance off the road and most appeared to be two-story farmhouses, with a few newer ranchers sprinkled among them.

"Mike should get here with the camera equipment tomorrow morning," Bill said, "so we'll be able to tape a show in the afternoon."

Good, thought Jillian. The busier she stayed, the less chance of getting involved with a certain mountain man.

Bill pulled to a stop in front of yet another white, two-story farmhouse. The front light gleamed a greeting and illuminated a cozy porch swing occupied by a large black dog.

The front door swung open, and a couple in their early sixties stepped onto the porch.

"We've been waiting for y'all," the woman said. Then she nudged her husband. "Lloyd, go help that girl with her suitcases."

Before long, they were settled in the Claytons' comfortable family room, watching home movies and getting to know one another. Jillian immediately felt as if she'd known the Claytons for ages.

She hadn't been crazy about the idea of coming here originally, and it was reassuring to know she'd be spending her time with such a kind, welcoming couple.

"It's so nice to finally meet this lovely young lady friend of Bill's that we've been hearing so much about," Mrs. Clayton gushed. "Do you know Julia Child?"

Jillian smiled, completely at home with the friendly couple. "No, but I wish I did."

"Me, too, honey. Why, I was telling Lloyd just the other day that I wish they still played her on TV.

'Course, your show is good, too. Our neighbor Mrs. Preston watches it everyday. She says it's just like 'Moonlighting' where you know that Cybill Shepherd and Bruce Willis have this thing going for each other, but you don't know when *they're* going to figure it out.''

Jillian darted a glance at Bill for his reaction and found him watching for hers.

She grinned, and he returned the expression with a telling wink. Though they hadn't spoken a word, they understood each other as clearly as if Jillian had said the words "I think I'm going to like it here" and Bill responded "I knew you would."

Jillian awoke in Bill's bedroom. Glancing around the high-ceilinged room, she took in the gun rack on the wall, the sports trophies on his dresser, and a picture of Bill and his sister taped to the wall mirror. He appeared to be about thirteen or fourteen, and his little sister was just a toddler.

She smiled as she remembered watching the movie images of a young Bill last night. The elder Claytons had provided a running commentary as the young boy played with his little sister, pitched a winning ball game and sang for the camera, using a broom handle as a stand-up microphone. Jillian knew then that Bill's hamminess had started at an early age.

Sunlight streamed past the blue curtains and spilled onto the patchwork quilt, beckoning Jillian to rise and greet the day. She got up, hastily pulled her warm robe about herself and ambled to the bathroom.

Pushing the door open, she was greeted by a billowing cloud of steam. Seconds later, when it cleared, she saw Bill standing there in all his glory.

He clapped his hands to his chest and gave a little "Eek!"

The motion attracted her attention to his chest where droplets beaded and glistened in curly golden hairs, then downward to the uncovered portion of his anatomy.

Jerking her eyes back up to meet his amused countenance, she fought the urge to about-face and run. "Excuse me," she said, pulling the robe tighter about herself, "I didn't realize the bathroom was occupied." With great restraint, she left, shutting the door tightly behind her.

"No problem," Bill called after her. "Stop in and see me anytime."

Last night she'd thought it odd to have a latch on the bedroom side of the door. This morning she understood and slid it into place. Bill chuckled at the sound.

Jillian hurriedly dressed in the chilly room. Couldn't the man be serious about anything? Did he always take everything as a joke?

Against her will, Jillian felt the corners of her mouth turn upward in a poorly suppressed smile. The more she thought about what had just happened, the more tickled she became. Only Bill Clayton would pretend modesty and cover his chest instead of . . . well, he certainly wasn't bashful. Recovered from her shock at seeing him in the altogether after his shower, Jillian had to admit once again that he certainly cleaned up well.

A drawer bumped closed in the next room, which Bill would share with Mike, and the next moment a tap sounded on her door leading to the hall. "The bathroom's all yours. Come on down to breakfast when you're through and then we'll go to the diner afterward."

There was no amusement in his voice now. She supposed if he ever got serious about anything, it was work. Even amid all his tomfoolery on the set, he was always dead serious about giving the viewers what they wanted. "I'll be down in five minutes," she said.

A few minutes later, her hair neatly in place and makeup flawless, Jillian opened the door to join the Clayton family downstairs. A large black dog, probably part Labrador, came forward and leaned against her leg. Then he sat on Jillian's shoe.

She eased her foot out from under the dog's bony bottom and patted him lightly on top of his head. The animal gave her a doggy smile and blinked in satisfaction with each pat.

"I smell bacon," she told the dog. "We'd better go eat before there's nothing left." Jillian started down the steps and turned to see the dog still sitting there, its furry brow knitted together in a perplexed frown as if to ask, "What are you doing here?"

"Beats me. If you figure it out before I do, let me know. Okay?"

The diner was a curious combination of gas station, luncheonette, pinball palace, social hall and gift shop. A smaller, separate building housed a laundry-shower facility for long-haul truckers, as well as a coin-operated water hose for washing cars.

Although the parking lot was well paved, several cars were parked on the grass, leaving an area clear under the basketball hoop that graced the side of the restaurant. Diners who parked their cars too close to the "court" risked a shattered windshield during the frequent games of one-on-one.

Bill told Jillian his parents had put up the hoop for him and his friends. Later, it came to be used to settle scores between agitated customers who wanted to "duke it out." When Lloyd Clayton told rowdies to take their arguments outside, their departure would soon be followed by the sound of a basketball hitting the side of the restaurant.

Inside, they were greeted by the delicious smells of breakfast from the kitchen and pot pourri from the gift shop. Lloyd and Peggy Ann Clayton had been here since five o'clock when the diner opened. It was a warm and friendly place, as were the smiles of the couple who greeted them.

"Belinda's ride didn't show up, so it'll be another half hour before she gets here," Mrs. Clayton told them. "Let me feed this breakfast crowd, then we can set up your camera."

"We'll be glad to help." Jillian put on an apron while Bill flashed her a strange look and followed suit. Maybe she should have spoken for herself, she supposed. But then she was pleased when he flashed her an approving smile.

Bill gathered up two of the shoe boxes she had set on the counter. "Let's put these in the office."

Jillian picked up the remaining box and followed him to the back of the diner. Even in an apron, he looked masculine. The long strings had been wrapped twice around his slim waist and tied in the back, the ends trailing down to caress the snug fit of his slacks.

Pushing aside a pile of clutter, Bill set the boxes on the scarred wooden desk. He took the box from Jillian, shook it slightly and frowned. "Too heavy for shoes."

"They're my recipes." Jillian opened the lid and removed a card. It was a yellowed newspaper clipping taped to an index card. A childish scrawl noted that "Daddy liked this."

Curious, Bill flipped through some of the others. Each noted the source: Grandma, *Texas Times* magazine, original, etc. And each had comments such as "Too dry" or "try with cinnamon next time." She had obviously been collecting these for many years. From the faraway look in her eyes, Bill could tell these scraps of paper meant a great deal to her.

He wondered if there was also a certain someone who meant a great deal to her. The mere thought of such a possibility rankled him. He pushed it from his mind.

Bill put the cards back in the shoe box. He wondered if, among all those cards and slips of paper, there was a recipe for a love potion. He wasn't much of a cook, but that was one recipe he'd be willing to try.

Even so, he wondered if a magic concoction could compensate for their differences. Jillian had told him she lived all over the country and for a couple of years in Germany while growing up. Until he had bought WXYZ and moved to Chesterfield County, he had always lived in Fullerton. Well, there were those four years at Virginia Tech, but he'd been so engrossed in his studies and his part-time job as campus radio announcer that he'd had little opportunity to soak up new experiences.

He wasn't ashamed of Fullerton. Perhaps the people in his community weren't as savvy or sophisticated as the people Jillian was used to, but they clung to good, old-fashioned values. Would she look past the roughness of their clothes and manners to see their kindness and generosity? Would she be able to look past his own twangy drawl and lack of fancy duds to recognize all that he had to offer?

Something told him she would. Having her here on his territory should ultimately prove that her primness was only an act. All she needed was the opportunity to be herself without anyone passing judgment on her. The people of Fullerton would surely give her that opportunity.

He slid the lid back onto the shoe box and pushed them to the corner of the desk. "These'll be safe here. Let's go help Mom before she sends a search party after us."

With Jillian helping on the grill, his father serving, and Bill bussing tables, the breakfast crowd thinned quickly. His parents were still laughing over Jillian's use of paprika on the fried eggs and parsley on the plates.

"I can see how people might think the paprika is different," Jillian said to Bill after cornering him in the kitchen, "but what's so funny about parsley?"

Bill scraped the plates and stacked them by the sink for Belinda to wash. He liked the way Jillian's cheeks flushed from standing over the grill. She had worked hard this morning, even though she'd been more creative than his parents were used to. "Around here, most people don't eat parsley unless they've had a nip or two and are trying to cover the smell on their breath."

"That is the craziest thing I ever heard." Jillian pushed her bangs off her damp forehead and followed him back out to the counter. "No, I take that back. Mr. Albritton's gravy on scrambled eggs is the craziest thing I've ever heard of."

She shook her head, but Bill could tell she was more amused than disgusted by Mr. Albritton's breakfast.

"Personally, I prefer gravy on my grits and biscuits."

Jillian smiled and gave a little grunt of disbelief.

"You know," said Bill, "maybe it would be a good idea to feature local guests on the show. You know, let them share their favorite recipes."

"Is this another of Susan's ideas?"

He needed to convince her that such a move would be good for the show. He had quickly discovered that people were more receptive to change if they understood the benefits associated with it.

"Yeah. She suggested we get back to basics. You can't get much more basic than Fullerton cooking."

"There's really no need," she said cheerfully. "I have recipes planned for the next two weeks."

"Then un-plan them. My mom can give you a list of the best cooks in the county."

Before she could utter a word of protest, Mrs. Preston broke in. "Well, if it ain't Bill Clayton. And Jill, too. What a nice surprise."

"Jillian," she responded with a warm smile and grasped the older woman's frail hand.

"Your show is my favorite soap opera. Why, I just love the way you two carry on so."

"Soap opera?" She looked at Bill who didn't seem to find anything unusual about Mrs. Preston's comment. "I'm afraid you're mistaken. 'Cooking With Jillian' isn't a soap opera."

The woman looked confused. "You mean you're not play-acting like Cybill Shepherd and Bruce Willis on those reruns of 'Moonlighting'?" She peered through the tops of her bifocals at both of them. "It's for a fact?"

It was one of those do-you-still-kick-your-dog kind of questions. No matter whether Jillian answered yes or no, she would be indirectly admitting that the fun and flirtation the woman saw on TV everyday was real. "It's a cooking show, that's all," Jillian said.

"Humph, could've fooled me."

Mrs. Preston, like many other locals who had heard about the happenings at Clayton's Kitchen, hung around to watch the taping. When Mr. and Mrs. Clayton offered advice during filming, Mrs. Preston and the other coffee-sipping customers felt inclined to put in their two cents' worth as well. Jillian found herself stopping frequently to jot down their excellent suggestions.

"I always put oatmeal in my meatloaf," offered Mrs. Preston.

"No, you should use cracker crumbs," said Memphis. He had arrived before noon, and he was encouraging, rather than discouraging, audience participation.

"I think Memphis wants a guest spot on the show," Bill teased. At least Jillian *thought* he was teasing.

"If you get Memphis on," Mrs. Preston piped in, "then you should ask Una Wilbur to make a pie out of her prize-winning rutabaga. That sucker's huge."

Bill flashed Jillian a see-I-told-you-it-was-a-good-idea grin.

Jillian felt as though she were being pushed into a corner. Mrs. Preston was a delightful woman, and if Una Wilbur was only half as nice as the people Jillian had met this morning, she was sure she'd adore her, too. But Bill's suggestion, though a good one, would lead them away from the original concept of the show.

She topped the meatloaf with strips of green pepper.

"It's very sweet of everyone to offer to help," she told Bill, "but before we make any more changes, we ought to consider whether these suggestions fit our show's format. Maybe we should talk about it later," she offered.

Bill glared at her. It was obvious he had expected her to go along with him, no questions asked. He was impulsive in his decisions, and Jillian thought it wise for one of them to consider the repercussions that would come from such a change. Although Bill kept up a running commentary with the spectators who filled the diner, he had little else to say to Jillian for the remainder of the show.

As he helped Mike carry the video equipment out to the van, he paused to joke with Mrs. Preston. The old gal was pushing ninety-three, but she still possessed enough energy to mow her own grass and keep up with all the gossip in the county. He carried an image of her, perched on the riding lawn mower, her skirt hiked up to her knees and stockings rolled down below them.

Then there was Custer Davis who made weird lawn art out of defective lumber and scraps of fabric. Although his house was on a busy straightaway, the speed limit had been lowered along the one-mile stretch to allow rubberneckers an opportunity to safely take in the strange sights in his yard before continuing on their way.

Yes, maybe they were a little odd, but who wasn't? They were his neighbors—his people—and Bill accepted all of them with or without their eccentricities. Despite their differences, it was clear that Jillian, too, was fond of these people that he loved.

He hoped she would learn to accept him, as well.

* * *

Jillian rolled out the biscuit dough for dinner and pressed the top of a glass into it.

"You didn't knead it too much, did you?" asked Mrs. Clayton. "Too much kneading makes the biscuits tough, sure as Christmas."

Jillian stood back to let the older woman inspect her work, then gave a satisfied smile at her nod of approval.

"You've been cooking all day. Why don't you go relax for a while? Bill's in the den watching the early news."

"Oh, I like cooking," Jillian said. "Especially when I share it with someone who enjoys it as much as I do." She lowered her eyes to the pan of biscuits. "Besides, I don't think Bill wants me around right now."

Mrs. Clayton stopped spooning brown sugar onto the corn squash to look Jillian squarely in the eye.

"He seems . . . perturbed."

"Don't pay him any mind. He's just distracted, that's all."

Jillian sighed.

"There's no need for you to fret," said Mrs. Clayton. "He gets like this when he's thinking about work. You should have seen him during the spell when he was trying to talk his daddy and me into opening the gift shop. The boy's a genius when it comes to marketing—that was his major in college. Sure enough, once we started selling arts and crafts and homemade sweets, our tourist business picked right up and truckers started buying gifts for their sweethearts and families."

Jillian nodded. "I guess you're right. He's been trying to convince me that we should feature guest cooks on the show."

"Now, that's not a bad idea."

"But down-home is not my style. You saw me putting paprika on the eggs. Besides, I never tasted souse or scrapple until this morning. How can I speak knowledgeably about something I'm not familiar with?"

"Sounds like you two've got some compromising to do."

Jillian considered Mrs. Clayton's statement as she lined a basket with a cloth napkin. She had already compromised by sharing her set with Boondock Bill. She didn't dare speculate what her serious-minded cooking instructor would think of such an arrangement.

Something furry pressed against her leg, then Jillian felt a weight on her foot. She looked down into soulful brown eyes. "You need to learn the difference between a shoe and a chair," she said, sliding her foot out from under the black dog.

"Just chase him out," said Mrs. Clayton. "That mooch started hanging around a few months ago. Bill fed him, and he's been here ever since."

The dog slowly blinked one eye as if sharing a secret with Jillian.

"He's not bothering me." Jillian emptied the pan of biscuits into the basket. One fell onto the counter and broke into three pieces. She picked up the smallest chunk and held it over the dog's head. With a conspiratorial wink, she dropped the warm bread. Strong canine jaws opened and closed with a snap. The mutt's expression never changed.

"I see you've met Frank." Bill stepped into the kitchen and snitched one of the biscuit fragments. "Mmm. Not bad."

"Who's Frank?"

"Him." Bill cupped the dog's jaw in his hands and turned it toward Jillian. "What else would you call someone with a face as sincere as that?" The mutt blinked sleepily.

"Yes, you're right," she admitted, smiling at the appropriateness of the name.

"Bill, if you're going to hang around the kitchen, you may as well wash your hands and set the table."

He saluted his mother, then flashed a lopsided grin at Jillian before doing her bidding.

Dinner in this close-knit family consisted of lots of good food and boisterous voices. Mike the cameraman and Memphis had also joined them for the meal. And Frank lay down at the corner of the table beside Jillian's chair as if hoping for more handouts. It was far different from the quiet, orderly dinners for three she had shared with her parents while growing up. In her family, the evening meal had been a time for somber discussions. Here, it was a time to catch up on gossip, outdo each other with wild tales and corny jokes, and even conduct arm-wrestling matches.

Despite all the commotion and varied conversations going on at once, Jillian felt her attention being drawn repeatedly to Bill who sat at right angles to her.

Beside him, Memphis engaged him in conversation. Bill's hands flew as he accentuated points with flamboyant gestures. Was this where he had developed his theatrics?

Lloyd Clayton mentioned that this gathering of six was small compared to the number that often joined them. "We never know who to expect at our table," he told Jillian. "Why, I remember one Sunday when all four of us, plus Memphis, invited a different family to eat with us after church. There must have been close to thirty people sitting all over the house with a plate on their lap.''

"Thirty people?" Jillian remembered the elegant dinner parties for eight that she had prepared for the Army officers her father frequently entertained. She usually started a week ahead by choosing a menu and ordering the floral centerpieces. "How did you plan for them?"

Mr. Clayton leaned back in his chair and pushed a thin strand of hair over his bald spot. "Honey, we don't plan much around here. It just sort of happens."

Mike took one of the two remaining biscuits. "There's one more. Anybody want it?"

Jillian groaned. "No thanks, I'm stuffed."

Strangely, Bill's parents and Memphis all turned to Bill. He had eaten at least three, so she couldn't imagine why they expected him to take another.

Bill looked up. He considered refusing it until Memphis, grinning like a mule eating briars, picked up the biscuit and held it just out of reach.

"Pass me the butter, Mike." Memphis dramatically smoothed his graying mustache in preparation for the tasty bread. "I'm really going to enjoy this *last* biscuit."

Bill picked at what was left of his fried chicken, pretending to ignore his pal's teasing. He was aware all eyes were on him. He kept trying to tell himself it didn't matter that Memphis would soon be eating the last biscuit and would reap the privilege associated with it. But, best friends or not, there were some things a man just didn't share.

Memphis smacked his lips and poked Bill in the ribs with his elbow. "Sure you don't want a bite, buddy?"

That did it.

Bill stood up, his chair scraping backward across the linoleum. Startled, Frank jumped to his feet and began barking. By now, Memphis was standing, and he and Bill were struggling for possession of the biscuit.

"Now, boys," said Mrs. Clayton.

Bill's father pulled out his wallet and handed his wife a ten-dollar bill. "Looks like you were right after all, Peggy Ann."

"I told you that boy has it bad."

Jillian caught Mike's eye, but he was just as puzzled as she. He looked uncertain whether to intervene between the two combatants.

The men grunted and huffed in their struggle. Bill had got the biscuit and held it out behind him, out of Memphis's reach.

Jillian stood up. "Bill, this is not the studio. We're in your parents' *home!*" She turned to Mr. Clayton. "What's going on? Please *do* something!"

The table lurched, and a fork clattered to the floor.

Mr. Clayton got up and started gathering dishes. "I *am* doing something. I'm getting the breakables out of the way."

Amid the shoving and barking, Mrs. Clayton rose to help her husband as if nothing out of the ordinary was happening. To Jillian, she said, "Whoever takes the last biscuit gets to kiss the cook." She shook her head. "They never fought like that over *my* last biscuit."

Chapter Six

Jillian supposed she should have been flattered about what happened last night. Never before had two men literally fought for the honor of kissing her.

Not that either of them had succeeded. Frank had won the privilege when he snatched the biscuit out of Bill's fingers. Before either Bill or Memphis realized what was happening, the dog had gobbled it down.

As Jillian soon learned, Memphis had merely been goading Bill last night. She couldn't help wondering if Bill had reacted out of possessiveness or competition.

She stirred the Newburg sauce in the double boiler. "Now's the time to add the lobster and sherry," she said to Bill as much as to the camera.

When he turned to hand her the ingredients, the camera lights emphasized the purple shiner at the outer edge of his eye.

Jillian cringed as she remembered the wallop he'd received when Memphis had made a fast grab for the biscuit at the same moment Bill bent to retrieve it from the dog.

Despite the vivid bruise of purple and blue—or perhaps because of it—Bill had refused makeup.

"How did you find a live lobster around these parts?" he asked. "It must've cost a fortune."

Jillian just smiled and measured out the sherry. She had learned not to discuss such a touchy subject with the cameras still rolling.

"Most people I know would never cook this stuff if they had to pay an arm and a leg for lobster," Bill insisted. "Can't they use something cheaper?"

"Crab or shrimp make excellent substitutes."

"How about catfish?"

Jillian stopped stirring to turn her full attention to Bill. It was often hard to tell whether he was teasing or serious.

"Well, I suppose, if the flavor doesn't overpower the—"

"Hey, Bill," Belinda called from where she stood wiping a table. "Where'd you get that black eye?"

That was all the invitation Bill needed. With a wink in Jillian's direction, he replied, "I tried to get a kiss from Miss Reed."

The diner erupted into laughter.

"This isn't the time or place," Jillian murmured to her sidekick. Her pleading look had no effect on him.

"She said she'd rather kiss a dog." Amid the ensuing mirth, Bill watched Jillian, his gaze settling on her mouth.

Even without a TV camera and restaurant full of customers, his intense stare would still have been disconcerting. Trying to regain control of the situation and lead the topic back to cooking, Jillian said, "This lobster Newburg is delicious served over toast or pasta."

But Bill continued staring at her mouth. Jillian self-consciously licked her lips. He reached toward her, his fingers touching her bottom lip as he removed an imaginary something. It was a gentle touch—almost erotic. Was he going to kiss her now, in front of twenty diners and a million TV viewers?

Bill looked down at his thumb and forefinger. "Humph. Just a speck of fuzz." With a mischievous grin, he added, "I thought it might have been a dog hair."

Playing along, Jillian put a hand on her hip. "If you don't stop teasing, I'm going to blacken your—"

"Coming through!" Mrs. Clayton pushed past with a large pan of chicken-fried steak.

Bill squeezed closer to Jillian to give his mother room to pass. "We need to find someplace else to film the show."

"You can use my kitchen," said Inez Strawderman. "We just got a new convection oven."

"What's your specialty?" Bill asked.

"I can make a mean batch of spoonbread."

"How about it, Jillian? What say we let Inez demonstrate her spoonbread for us?"

He'd cornered her and given her no way out. Jillian squirmed under his sneaky tactics. How could she refuse his suggestion with all these people watching and not look like the villain?

She gave Inez a smile and turned to Bill. "I'd love to hear about Inez's spoonbread, but our time is almost up, so let's talk about that after the show." To the camera she said, "Next time, we'll make Halloween treats for your favorite pooch. Be sure to tune in next week for Canine Crunchies."

Bill made a noise that sounded like air escaping from an overfilled tire. "A dog would be more thrilled with the fat from your steak."

"We'll let Frank be the judge of that."

When the show was finished, Bill decided they could double up and tape another. Because of her stage fright, Jillian worked best by writing out the recipes in large letters on oversize index cards. Since she hadn't prepared ahead for the doggie-treat recipe, Mrs. Clayton filled in by demonstrating her version of chicken and dumplings.

The second taping went well. Mrs. Clayton was a delightful guest, despite the crowded restaurant. Her enthusiasm rivaled her son's. She did, however, tend to take over the show, giving orders to both Jillian and Bill. Jillian saw this as vivid proof that Bill came by these traits naturally.

Honest faults or not, she couldn't let him keep making decisions about the show without consulting her first. It was too disruptive, no matter how fun, having guests on the set.

The next day, after church, she decided to bring up the subject with him. Actually it had already been brought up in church. Many times, in fact. It seemed word got out that there was a casting call for guest spots on her show, and every star-struck cook in the county wanted to be discovered.

Changing out of her dress and into slacks, Jillian happened to look out the bedroom window at the beautiful mountainous scenery that loomed on the landscape. A motion in the well-groomed yard caught her attention. Frank casually loped past, picked up a length of frayed rope in his teeth, and carried it to Bill, prompting a spirited game of tug-of-war.

Even at play, Bill gave no less than a hundred percent. He didn't even give slack to a dog. Bill forced Frank to fight for every inch of ground he won.

Jillian realized he'd done the same to her. And it was obvious she'd have to continue struggling against him to make the show the kind of success she wanted it to be.

With Quint, she'd meekly given in and gone along with his desires. And look where that had got her. Three years behind in her life plan, that was where.

It went against her nature, pushing back when she'd been shoved into a tight spot, but with Bill she had no choice. The man could be a human steamroller at times, and she refused to be flattened by him. She got out a warm jacket and pulled it on, then went outside to Bill.

By the time she walked around to the side of the house, both man and dog were breathless. She had no idea who won, for they were now sitting side by side on the cool autumn ground, Bill with his arm slung affectionately around the dog, and Frank with his tongue lolling out one side of his mouth.

Frank noticed her first. He left his master and greeted Jillian by nuzzling her hand.

Bill rose to his feet. "Traitor," he said to the dog.

Jillian patted her new friend and told Bill, "I don't know whether he likes me more for my biscuits or my kisses."

Bill grinned. It was clear what his preference would be.

Jillian's thoughts darted back to that last kiss they'd shared. Powerful. Mind-drugging. Lusty. All the things a kiss should be—between two people in love.

But they weren't in love. They weren't even right for each other. It just happened that she was illogically attracted to him.

A more logical choice for Jillian would be a three-piece-suit type, a doctor perhaps, a local politician, or possibly a military officer. Thanks to her unfortunate experience with Quint, she no longer included lawyers on her list of compatible types.

He was watching, waiting for her to say something. His heavy-lidded look undermined her and made her feel more like loving than fighting.

She'd have to stop thinking like this. It wouldn't be fair to either of them. Jillian gritted her teeth. As far as Jillian was concerned, her dealings with Bill Clayton must be business only. With a business-only attitude, there was less risk of damaging her career—or her heart.

"I came out here to tell you—" Jillian purposely lowered her voice to make her statement sound more authoritative "—that I can't allow guest chefs on the 'Cooking With Jillian show.'"

Bill stared at her for a moment, as if stunned that she hadn't changed her mind in the past couple of days. "I'm real sorry you feel that way, but we've already spread the word that we're looking for people."

"No, *you* spread the word. Bill, guests just don't fit well into our format." Frank nudged her hand, hinting for a scratch behind the ears. Jillian obliged him, then spoke again. "I'm the chef on this show. You're the entertainment. We agreed on that. There isn't room for anyone else."

"All right, I'll be blunt," Bill said, stepping closer. "Most people don't cook the kind of food you've been preparing. Not unless they're having company, that is.

Most of our viewers are interested in pepping up their own everyday meals.''

"Food shouldn't have to be ordinary just because it's for family. Why save the good stuff for company?''

Exasperated, Bill grabbed her by the shoulder. He couldn't help it, but his voice rose along with his frustration. "Why can't you understand that having guests will be good for the show? Do you honestly believe people want to cook a bunch of stuff they can't even pronounce?''

A low rumble erupted beside Jillian. Bill looked down to see Frank, ears laid flat and teeth bared. He released her shoulder, and she rubbed where he had gripped.

"I wasn't going to hurt her, Benedict Arnold,'' he mumbled to the dog. At that, Frank hung his head and looked contrite.

Bill couldn't blame the animal for trying to protect her. Hadn't he done the same when he thought she was in danger of being hurt by a bomb? He looked at the dog gazing adoringly at Jillian. *So you see through her, too?* Even Frank sensed she needed a friend, and maybe protection from time to time.

She was vulnerable. Never mind that she could be as crisp as cucumbers at times, Bill knew she was more fragile than she wanted anyone to know.

He might not be able to protect her. Heck, he doubted she'd even want protection from anyone. The least he could do was be a friend to her.

Her arms lay folded across her chest. It was a defensive posture, and she didn't like feeling defensive around Bill. Consciously relaxing her stance, Jillian relented but would not give in completely. "I'm trying to see things your way, but I'd like you to consider my position, too. I'm willing to use your friends' recipes occasionally, but having a third person on the show could ruin our successful formula. I don't want to risk that."

"I won't force the issue," Bill said, "but I believe you'll come around to my way of thinking before long."

All Jillian could do was gape. What had just happened? She'd been prepared to deliver the next point of debate, yet he'd given in. Just like that.

He must be up to something.

Bill smiled, making the slight cleft in his chin more noticeable. The simple gesture made her uneasy. "You'd better close your mouth if you don't want to catch flies," he said.

Belatedly Jillian snapped her jaw shut and turned to walk to the house.

Mrs. Clayton came onto the front porch. "Bill! Telephone."

"Who is it?" he asked as they approached his mother.

"Some woman from Richmond. I didn't catch her name."

She stood in the hall, taking off her coat while Bill talked on the phone.

"Next Saturday? Sounds like fun, but I had something else in mind for that night."

It must be his girlfriend, she thought. She couldn't imagine a man like Bill *not* having lots of girlfriends. Quint, being the charmer that he was, had also had his share of girlfriends, even after marriage.

Though she had only known him a short time, Jillian was convinced that Bill would be a good husband to some lucky woman. Whether he had one girlfriend now or a hundred, she was certain he would do right by the woman he ultimately committed himself to.

But that was none of her concern.

Jillian hung her coat on the wall peg and went upstairs to her room. Bill's room. What irony that she should be sleeping in Bill's bed while he carried on a long-distance romance with another woman.

Not that she cared. She shouldn't care, actually, but for some odd reason she felt like a piece of her had just shriveled up inside.

So what if Bill had a date? That had nothing to do with her. Jillian had other goals, and because of them, her priorities did not include men—least of all, handsome mountain men.

Well, she refused to cloister herself in this room for the rest of the afternoon. With a fresh focus on her priorities, she decided to go back to the diner and prepare tomorrow's recipes. Doing so would serve the dual purpose of moving toward her goal of making her reputation as a fine chef and keeping an adequate distance between her and Bill.

She opened the bedroom door and collided with Bill's hard torso. His hands reached out and clasped her upper arms, steadying her as she reflexively jumped back.

"Whoa, what's the hurry?"

His hands stayed on her arms. Jillian was so aware of his touch, she imagined she could feel each individual ridge of his fingerprints through her sleeve. Taking a calming breath, she tugged the bottom of her blouse to straighten it. "Don't you ever knock?"

It was a ridiculous question, for she had been the one to open the door and crash into him. Taking the offense position always worked well when she was feeling defensive.

The vertical lines between Bill's eyebrows disappeared as he took in the absurdity of her question. One corner of his mouth hitched slightly upward.

"Pardon me," he said. "If I had known you would come barging out into the hall like that, I would have worn my baseball catcher's vest."

His comment drew her eyes to his chest, where soft brown hairs peeked from the vee of his shirt. And that reminded Jillian of the last time she'd opened the door on him, when those chest hairs had glistened with water droplets from his shower.

Her cheeks burned at the memory. He seemed to be enjoying the moment so much she automatically responded with her tried-and-true tactic.

"Did you come up here for a reason?"

Smiling even more broadly, he asked, "You going downstairs?" When she nodded, he tucked her hand into the crook of his elbow and walked down with her.

"Susan wanted us to go to her Halloween party next Saturday," he said.

"Us?"

"Yeah, she and her husband are inviting all of her clients to this party. They thought it would be a kick to have Boondock Bill and Jillian."

Unexpectedly Jillian breathed a little sigh of relief. Then, when she realized that she was relieved because Bill hadn't been talking to a girlfriend, she gave herself a mental shake. *Get a grip,* she told herself. *You have no concern with Bill's love life. Concentrate on the matter at hand.*

"What do we wear to this party?" she asked.

"I told her we couldn't go." They reached the bottom step, and Bill turned to face her. "I was hoping you'd go with me to the Halloween square dance over in Truxton."

His expression was so earnest, Jillian almost said yes immediately. But then she remembered how quickly he'd given in to her earlier when she'd insisted they have no guest cooks on the show. *You'll come around to my way of thinking,* he'd said. Was this invitation part of his plan to win her over to his views? More likely, he was getting her out among the public so *they* could put the pressure on her.

"If we're going to continue taping two or three shows a day, as you suggested," she said, "then I don't see how we'll have the time."

"We'll make time."

The way he said it, his voice soft and husky, implied that his statement held more than one meaning. Again, the image of Bill emerging from the shower invaded her mind.

He stood a few inches taller than Jillian, which put her eyes just above his chin level. His lips were wide and firm, yet pliable, leading her to wonder what it would be like to "make time" with Bill Clayton.

"Say you'll go with me," he insisted.

"I don't know how to square-dance."

"I'll teach you."

"Do I need a costume?"

"You can wear my sister's—she's about your size." Bill rubbed his chin. "Are you always this spontaneous?"

His teasing struck a raw spot inside. Jillian had always been methodical, thanks in large part to her father's military influence. But the main reason she tried so hard to plan every aspect of her life was so she wouldn't be caught off guard. If she knew what to expect, she could have a mental script ready for the occasion.

Jillian opened her mouth to say something witty in response, but nothing came to mind.

"I'll take that as a yes."

She nodded in affirmation, hoping this wouldn't be a mistake. "Um, I'm going to walk up to the diner and start preparing for tomorrow's taping."

"I'll drive you," he offered.

"Thanks, but I need the exercise."

"Then take my bicycle. It's too far to walk."

A few minutes later, Bill watched her ride away from him, her shapely derriere moving from side to side as she stood to pedal faster up the incline.

It gave him a feeling of satisfaction whenever he came home and stopped long enough to survey the beauty of the surroundings. In his possessiveness, he claimed the rolling countryside as his own, as well as the hardpacked dirt road, the rusted blue bike, and even the leggy brunette.

He didn't own her any more than he owned the river flowing through Fullerton Valley, but that didn't stop him from wanting to claim her. Bill considered the different ways in which he could claim Miss Jillian Reed. He already had her as his employee and cohost. Yet, more than once, he'd wanted to possess her body. He'd start with those prim lips that seemed perpetually pressed into a thin horizontal line, and kiss them until they softened. Then he'd work his way down the length of her, all the way to her toes, kissing and exploring as he went.

But he wanted more than just her body, or her presence beside him at work. He wanted to claim her heart.

It seemed only fair since she'd already stolen his.

* * *

Lloyd Clayton smiled at Jillian from behind the grill, and she returned the greeting as she walked past him toward the office. Although it was not yet four o'clock, he was already preparing for the Sunday dinner regulars.

Jillian pushed the office door open. Inside, Belinda jumped and hurriedly closed the closet door.

"Jillian! What are you doing here? I mean, you startled me."

"Oh, I'm sorry," Jillian soothed the teenager. "Don't mind me. I'll just get my recipes and go to a booth to prepare for tomorrow's tapings."

"Uh, I was just finishing up in here. Why don't you sit at the desk?" Belinda suggested. "I'll close the door behind me."

Jillian sat and pulled the battered shoe boxes toward her. Surprised at how light they felt, she opened each one, only to discover all three were empty.

Quickly she searched through the clutter on the desk, then pulled drawers open to see if they'd been stashed in there. A flash of panic swept over her. What could have happened to all those recipe cards?

Belinda had picked up her broom and dust rag and was on her way out when Jillian stopped her.

"Have you seen my recipe cards?"

"Aren't they in those shoe boxes?"

"No, and I can't imagine where they might be." Jillian's voice rose in desperation.

"I wouldn't worry about it if I were you. They'll probably turn up in a few days."

"I can't wait a few days. I have to find them *now*."

Belinda mumbled something and shut the door behind her.

A lot of help she was. Jillian went back out to the diner to question Mr. Clayton, but he hadn't seen them, either.

"I could understand if the boxes had been misplaced," said Jillian, "but it's as if someone must have emptied them on purpose."

"Now, honey, I don't think anybody *took* your recipes. They must be around here someplace."

Until he'd mentioned it, Jillian hadn't considered the possibility that someone might have stolen them.

Who would want to steal recipe cards? If she were famous, she might suspect they had been stolen for souvenirs.

Perhaps the thief hoped to publish them in a cookbook as she had already planned to do. No, that seemed a little far-fetched.

Jillian wondered who would be motivated to take her cards. Was it because, without her own recipes, Jillian would be forced to turn to others for help?

Had one of the locals wanted so desperately to be on the show that she or he would stoop to such measures? Jillian didn't think so. The people she'd met in Fullerton struck her as honest and forthright. And although she knew Bill shared those qualities, she couldn't help recalling his words: *You'll come around to my way of thinking.*

She doubted this was his way of making her "come around," but still she had to know for sure.

"I'm sure they didn't just up and walk away," said Mr. Clayton. "We'll help you find them."

"Thanks, but I think I know where they might be."

Outside, Bill pulled up and parked beside the bike rack. He was glad Mike had suggested they come up for a game of Foosball. It gave him a good excuse to hang around until Jillian finished whatever she was doing to prepare for tomorrow's taping. Then he could offer her a ride home or maybe take her for a drive.

He followed Mike inside. Jillian stood with her back to them as she pulled her jacket on. "Finished already?" Bill asked. "Wait for me to find Mike a Foosball opponent, and I'll give you a ride home."

She turned around and stared a hole through him. Those pale blue eyes were questioning as she approached him.

To Mike, he said, "There's Ken Tolbert. He's always open for a fast game of Foosball."

"Sure thing." Mike excused himself to the game room.

"Bill, I can't seem to find my recipe cards. You didn't put them anywhere, did you?"

Bill heard Belinda mutter, "Uh-oh."

"Someone has removed them from the boxes they were in."

He clenched his jaw. "And you think I took them?"

"I thought it could have been your way of trying to persuade me to have guest cooks on the show."

"If I want to persuade a woman to do something," he told her through gritted teeth, "I don't have to resort to underhanded tricks."

Chapter Seven

During taping the next day, both Bill and Jillian were cool and reserved. Jillian hadn't meant to offend Bill by asking if he knew anything of their whereabouts. But the more she had tried to explain herself, the worse the situation had become. And now she was faced with the prospect of cohosting the show in an atmosphere charged with angry tension.

Memphis, however, made up for their lack of playfulness.

"Thanks for agreeing to do the show with us at the last minute," Bill told his friend.

"No problem. It's a good thing I went hunting this weekend and got something to cook for y'all."

"Oh, heavens," said Jillian.

"You'll like roast possum," Memphis assured her. "Especially the way I cook it."

She caught Bill watching her and willed herself not to grimace. Jillian tied on an apron. "Let's hurry up and get this over with."

The camera started rolling, and Memphis soon launched into the story of how he had bagged the possum.

Jillian felt as though she were losing all control of the show. This was a cooking show, not "The Wild Kingdom"! To get Memphis off the subject of what kind of shot he used, she asked him, "Aren't you going to wear a hair net?"

He touched the straggly ends of his shoulder-length hair. "I suppose I could, if you really want me to." Then Memphis turned and hollered to someone off camera. "Hey, you got a rubber band?" He left them while he attended to his hair.

Jillian sighed heavily while Bill snickered at his friend's antics. "Now do you see why I said having guests was a bad idea?" she asked before remembering that the camera was still focused on them.

Memphis came back and smiled to the camera. His graying hair was now held back in a short ponytail at the base of his neck.

"What about your beard?" Jillian persisted. She realized she was taking her frustration out on Memphis when it was the misplaced recipe cards that had upset her.

"I ain't putting my beard in no ponytail!"

"Memphis," Bill interjected, "she was joking. Why don't you tell us how to cook a possum?"

Memphis turned out to be almost as big a ham as Bill. With a mischievous grin, he said, "Well, first you want to get one without tread marks..."

From that point on, he took over the show.

Fortunately the next few days brought guests who, though just as lovable and entertaining as Memphis, were less inclined to show off. Once word got out that they were having local cooks on the show, they had a long list of people anxious to demonstrate their culinary skills.

Bill and Jillian had reached an uneasy truce. Bill's horsing around on the set now involved the guest cook instead of Jillian.

Jillian was just as glad, for it allowed her to focus on presenting the recipes with a professional demeanor. The third person on the show also served as a buffer between them. But, still, she missed the lighthearted camaraderie they had once shared.

Things went pretty smoothly with the school teacher and her Halloween spider cookies, the firefighter and his three-alarm chili, and the church ladies with their bake-sale confections.

They even had one of Bill's relatives on the show. "My second cousin, twice removed," Bill had quipped, "but he kept coming back."

Though she hadn't expected it to happen, Jillian fell in love with the people of this close-knit community. Who wouldn't? she thought as she recalled how they had included her in local get-togethers as well as inviting her into their homes.

By the week's end, Jillian begrudgingly admitted, if only to herself, that it had been a good idea to invite guests onto the show. They had even started taping the programs in their guests' homes.

Their last guest that week was her favorite. At ninety-two, Mrs. Preston had amassed a wealth of cooking tips and shortcuts. And since she had lived longer than most folks in Fullerton, she felt free to say whatever was on her mind. That included dispensing advice about their program.

"You always cook those fancy meals that people only serve to important company," Mrs. Preston told Jillian while taping.

Jillian braced herself for the inevitable. She briefly wondered if Bill had talked to the elderly woman about this since he'd already mentioned that her recipes were too "highfalutin."

"And you," the elderly woman said to Bill, "you always want to do everyday meals. Why don't y'all make everyone happy by giving the plain and fancy versions of all your recipes?"

Jillian caught Bill's eye over the tiny lady's head. He looked as surprised as she was at the suggestion.

"For instance, I'm going to cook my blue-ribbon pumpkin pie today. Now, if you want to dress it up for company, you just pour the same filling into these teeny tart shells and decorate them with whipped cream and fruit slices."

"That's a wonderful idea," said Jillian. And it was simple, too. This way, she and Bill could have their cake and eat it, too, so to speak. In fact, that's exactly what she'd done when Bill had asked about cheaper substitutes for lobster in the Newburg recipe. "Mrs. Preston, you're a genius."

The older woman looked as though she'd never doubted that assessment for a minute. "Of course I'm right," she agreed. "Now, step aside so I can start my pie."

Later, after they'd packed the camera in Mike's car and carried out the leftover pie that Mrs. Preston had insisted they take with them, Bill took the road heading away from his parents' house.

"Forget your way?" Jillian teased.

He gave a half smile and shrugged.

He wasn't usually this quiet, and Jillian wasn't sure how to handle his silence. She realized she'd become accustomed to his easy banter and corny jokes. It surprised her that she actually missed his boisterousness. She had once wished he'd conduct himself with more restraint; now that her wish had come true, this new behavior unsettled her.

To break the uneasy silence, Jillian started talking about the first subject that popped into her mind.

"I thought the shows went very well this week."

Bill glanced at her, then looked quickly back at the road. "Too bad we had guest cooks, or it would have gone even better, huh?"

"No, I..." It was hard for Jillian to admit when she was wrong, but she couldn't lie to him. "I think the people of Fullerton were wonderful. They made a definite improvement. You were right about that." Then she conceded, "It might even be good to continue the practice occasionally."

She sat back against the vinyl seat, waiting for him to gloat or make some wisecrack. He didn't comment at all.

"I still haven't found my recipe cards." As soon as she said it, Bill stiffened.

"I'll get your cards back for you," he ground out.

She wondered how he planned to do it. For now, she wouldn't question him about this promise. "Thank you."

For the next ten minutes, neither spoke a word as they drove along potholed roads past a creek, rocky hillsides and homes that jutted out of the countryside at

sporadic intervals. Jillian studied the view as she pon-
dered the man beside her.

Bill Clayton was full of surprises—first, with his
spontaneous tomfoolery, and now with his sudden silence. She really couldn't blame him for being upset
with her. Though she hadn't meant it that way, her
question about the disappearance of the cards had
sounded like an accusation.

"Where are we going?" she asked.

"To the river. There's a clearing that would make a
great spot for an outdoor cooking segment."

Jillian's first impulse was to protest, but considering
her misjudgment on his last idea, she decided to at least
hear him out on this one.

He pulled up and parked behind a canoe-outfitter's
shack, then they followed a narrow path to semi-flat
ground near the river's edge.

Old campfires had blackened the area inside a circle
of large, smooth stones, and a thick log had obviously
been dragged to the campsite to serve as a bench. A
closer look disclosed a discarded wire coat hanger that
must have once been used for roasting hot dogs or
marshmallows. Water babbled in the stream, and a cool
breeze groped its way under the back of Jillian's jacket.
She rubbed her arms.

"Don't you think it's rather cold for a cookout?"

"Hunters don't think so. The cooler it is, the less
chance of game picking up their scent. After a day of
tracking animals, they camp out and get an early start
the next morning."

"Ugh. Don't tell me you hunt, too. I thought I'd get
sick thinking about that poor opossum Memphis shot."

He flashed her a teasing grin. "I thought you liked
roast possum with sweet potatotes."

Jillian pushed her hands into her jacket pockets. "It was okay—a little greasier than I expected. You didn't answer my question. Do you hunt?"

He seemed reluctant to answer. "I did a few times—mostly squirrels and rabbits." Bill sat on the log, picked up the wire, and started poking among the ashes. "I'd rather shoot tin cans off the back fence."

"What about that deer head in your living room? Didn't you kill it?"

He chuckled. "No, my father shot it. Mom didn't mind cooking the venison, but she refused to hang the trophy over the fireplace. So I use it as a drying rack."

Jillian moved closer to the log bench, but she didn't sit. "I can't believe it. A country boy who doesn't hunt."

Bill's eyes darkened.

Immediately Jillian regretted teasing him. It might be a sore spot for him, she reasoned, especially if, in Fullerton, hunting was considered a rite of passage into manhood. Maybe he'd already received much ribbing about his lack of enthusiasm for killing wild animals. Had his friends called him a wimp? Even if they had, she knew they couldn't have believed such a preposterous thought.

He stood, looming over her more in attitude than proximity. "There seem to be a number of things about me you have difficulty believing."

Bill turned away, tilting his head slightly to one side as if listening to the sound of the breeze rustling the crisp autumn leaves.

"I had hoped that by coming here for a couple of weeks we'd get to know each other better," he continued. "Learn to trust each other. It's important to have trust when you work as closely as we do."

"I trust you." In the short time she'd known him, Jillian had discovered Bill to be an honorable man—one who played by the rules. If she was in a situation that required it, she would trust him with her life.

"Do you?"

The simple question seemed to echo in her ears. "Of course I do."

Quint had manipulated her with sweet talk. Just because he'd been a conniving son of a gun, it was no reason to think Bill wouldn't be totally aboveboard and honest. Her friends at the time of the divorce had been wrong. All men were not alike. And she'd been wrong to expect manipulation tactics from Bill just because her ex-husband had been that way.

"I never *really* thought you had anything to do with my recipes' disappearance. I guess I panicked." Quietly she added, "I'm sorry I offended you."

When his expression softened, she knew he had forgiven her.

"If we're going to continue to work together," Bill said, "we need to be a team. That means we both play on the same side."

"No team captain?"

"I pay your salary."

Jillian smiled. He was teasing her again, which meant he was letting bygones be bygones. "But I'm the chef." She rubbed her arms again and stamped her foot against the chill.

Bill slipped an arm around her shoulders, and they started walking back to the car.

Jillian enjoyed the closeness. She also liked the forgiveness. He had forgiven her, even though her apology had come much too late. In her eyes, he grew six inches taller.

"Bill," she said, "I'm sorry I misjudged you. I've been burned before, and it's made me overly defensive."

He squeezed her shoulder in reply. "I never wanted anything of yours, Jillian. Nothing but your—"

Jillian waited for him to finish, but he seemed to have become lost in thought. "My what?"

Their feet crunched on gravel. They were back at the car. Bill opened the passenger door, then blocked the entrance. "Your cooperation," he said finally.

The way he said it, his eyelids at half-mast and one hand still resting on her waist, was enough to make Jillian cooperate in anything he suggested. She knew he'd been referring to their work. At least, that was what their discussion had been about. But his body language was referring to after-hours cooperation.

Her body happily obliged. It molded perfectly to his physique as he held her close. When he kissed her, Jillian responded with a warmth that belied the sharp October air.

He tasted vaguely of pumpkin pie with nutmeg. Bill kissed her again and lifted his head. His eyes gleamed. "I like this kind of teamwork."

"Mmm."

He gave her an affectionate pat on the backside. "What say we come back here tomorrow and do an outdoor-cooking piece?"

"Sounds like a good idea." And she meant it.

Saturday turned out to be an Indian summer day as temperatures rose to the upper sixties. Jillian dressed casually in a pink sweat suit and sneakers. Her usual attire of a smart dress and heels would be ridiculously out of place on the riverbank.

One of Memphis's hunting buddies had agreed to share his camping recipes. Not surprisingly, they turned out to be beans and franks. To keep things interesting, Jillian decided to cook a fish, using one of her simpler recipes that she'd committed to memory.

While Vernon clattered about with his tin cooking utensils and readied the fire, Jillian wrapped the trout Bill had caught that morning in cheesecloth, and doused it thoroughly with lemon juice.

Now that the air had been cleared between them, Bill and Jillian were once again exchanging teasing insults.

"You two are a regular Sonny and Cher today, aren't ya?" the older man asked.

Not quite, thought Jillian. Sonny had never looked at Cher the way Bill looked at her now. She lightly brushed her face with the back of her hand, fearing she would find a stray bit of egg from breakfast. Nothing seemed out of place. She hadn't really thought she'd been wearing egg, but Bill had been watching her so intently. His attention both pleased and discomfitted her. Jillian felt herself blushing under his perusal.

His gaze shot past her toward the thatch of woods behind her. "Do either of you have a recipe for rabbit?"

Everyone turned in the direction where Bill was staring. Frank emerged from the underbrush, carrying something limp and brown in his mouth.

"Oh, Bill, he killed that poor little rabbit!" Suddenly Jillian wasn't quite as fond of the black dog as she'd originally believed herself to be. She turned to Bill and whacked him with a wad of cheesecloth. "Why did you have to bring him here?"

He clutched his arm, pretending to be injured. "I'm glad you didn't have a knife in your hand."

"I got stabbed with a barbecue fork once," Vernon volunteered.

Frank pranced to the set and sat on Jillian's shoe.

"Ooh, he's wet!"

"Must have gone swimming," Bill offered.

Jillian pulled her foot out from under the dog, who proudly deposited his furry bundle on the ground in front of her. He grinned his doggy grin at her as if expecting praise, or at least a pat on the head. When none was forthcoming, he nudged the rabbit with his nose.

"I think he wants it to run so he can chase it again," Vernon said.

Bill picked up the rabbit and turned it over in his hands. "It's breathing. See, its chest is moving."

The rabbit jerked. Tiny feet clawing furiously, it scrambled out of Bill's hands and dashed off into the woods.

Jillian grabbed Frank's collar. The dog's momentum knocked her to her knees before she pulled him to a halt.

Bill came to her, offering a hand up. Jillian reached up to grab his hand. Then she saw the long red scratches on his wrists. "Bill, you're hurt."

"Yeah, he clawed me good. Faked me out, fainting like that. I didn't expect him to come to so fast."

"You should wash the wounds so they won't get infected." No one had thought to bring fresh water—just hot coffee in a thermos—so Jillian dug through her purse until she found a towelette in a foil packet. "Here, this should kill the germs."

"Ow! That stings. They put lemon juice in those things."

"Don't be a baby." She finished wiping his arms. They were strong and wiry, with prominent veins and corded muscles. Dark hair covered his arms, and Jillian enjoyed the way it tickled her hand as she tended to the scratches.

"Hey, y'all, the beans and hot dogs are ready," said Vernon. "But I'm not so sure about this fish that's all wrapped up like a mummy."

"My trout! I forgot all about it. I hope it's not overcooked."

"What about the claw marks? Aren't you going to kiss them and make them better?"

Jillian wondered what he would do if she actually took him up on his request. He'd probably revel in it, camera or no camera. She remembered the last time he'd asked her to kiss an injury and make it better. His invitation had been quite clear. And Jillian's emotional response had been embarrassingly obvious. Perhaps, in this case, humor would be her best defense.

"I hear dog saliva contains healing elements. Perhaps Frank will kiss it for you."

When he heard his name, Frank stopped digging at the base of a nearby tree and tilted both ears toward Jillian.

"No thanks," said Bill. "It's not the same."

"Here, hold this." Jillian handed him a large platter. Now, all she had to do was gently roll the fish out onto the plate.

It plopped with such force, the head broke loose, and a round black object fell off the plate. The thing rolled a short distance across the log bench, then fell into the dirt.

Vernon stopped stirring his beans and leaned over to gawk at it. "Gross," he said.

"Shoot! It's overcooked."

Mike was laughing so hard he stepped away from the tripod to keep from shaking the camera. The lens remained zoomed in on the errant fish eye.

"It's not your fault, honey," Bill reassured. "This fish has never been out of the river before. It's probably just—" Bill burst into a fit of laughter and doubled over, clutching his waist "—taking a look around!"

Jillian took the plate from Bill. If this had happened a month ago, she would have been mortified. Today, however, it was all she could do to hold back a chuckle. The man was absolutely crackers. He must go through life waiting for something bizarre to happen so he could make a wisecrack like that. Jillian mentally commended him for his quick wit, then lost her composure.

Her shoulders shaking with mirth, she sat on the log. After a moment, she blotted the moisture from her eyes with her sleeve.

Bill sat beside her and congratulated himself. Not long ago, he'd vowed to wipe that tight-lipped, prim smile off her face and replace it with a genuine smile. He'd succeeded. And he liked it better than he ever imagined possible.

"How about a taste of that fish?" He would rather have a taste of those smiling pink lips, but there would be time for that later. Maybe after the square dance tonight.

"The heck with the fish," Vernon groused. "What about my beans and hot dogs?"

They'd forgotten forks, too, so Bill broke a piece off with his fingers. "Mmm, pretty good." He broke off another morsel and fed it to Jillian.

Mike motioned that their time was almost up, so they each took a hot dog and tin cup full of beans from Vernon. After tasting each and complimenting the older man, they said their farewells to the camera.

Afterward Mike joined them for an outdoor lunch. The hot dog was burnt on the outside and cold inside. Bill ate it and the cup of beans in silence, watching Jillian as she carried on a spirited conversation with Mike and Vernon.

Jillian was talking about something that had happened at the station, punctuating her comments by pointing and gesturing with her half-eaten hot dog. As Mike told some of the pranks the cameramen had pulled on one another, Jillian listened with rapt attention, forearms resting against her crossed knee. She seemed unaware of Frank who, at that moment, sniffed her food and took a tentative lick.

Emboldened by her lack of response, the dog nibbled off a corner of the bun, then progressed upward to where Jillian's fingers grasped the final bit. Almost imperceptibly, her fingers opened, dropping the last bite into Frank's eager chops. When she moved, her gaze caught Bill's.

"My goodness," she quipped, "it's a dog-eat-dog world, isn't it?"

Bill groaned at her pun. Their gazes held. He admired the way her eyes danced with merriment, and he warmed to her sense of the ridiculous as they shared a quiet moment of camaraderie. Yes, indeed, she'd come a long way.

"Don't give me that," he said, grinning. "You purposely let Frank take your frank."

Jillian smiled her response.

In a smooth motion, she rose to pour a cup of coffee from the thermos. Bill watched, transfixed, as she carefully measured out the cup of coffee so as not to spill any. Bill noted with appreciation the way the pink sweatpants hugged her rounded bottom. The pink-and-gray knit top she wore was one of those unshaped numbers that relied on the wearer to provide the form. And she certainly did.

Though the outfit was modest, Bill's thoughts were not. He let his eyes travel hungrily over her curves and down the length of her well-shaped legs. His imagination filled in what was so carefully concealed, and Bill thought how much he liked the color pink. Especially on her.

"I said, would you like some coffee?" Jillian placed a hand on one pink hip and turned toward him.

Mesmerized by the gentle swells and valleys of her body, Bill was vaguely aware of her voice. It wasn't until Mike leaned over and nudged him with an admonishment to "wake up" that he shook himself free of her spell. Meeting her eyes, he saw from her expression that she'd been aware of his thorough perusal.

"Uh, yeah," he said, licking his dry lips. "I could use something hot."

Jillian had been tempted to give Bill the coffee sans a cup—right in his lap.

It had been obvious to Jillian that he'd been staring at her with a hunger that no amount of hot dogs and beans could satisfy. She had been attempting to ignore the physical reaction his perusal aroused in her and pretend he was merely distracted. And then he'd popped out that comment that let everyone know for certain where his thoughts had been.

Sliding the gold snake bracelet above her elbow, Jillian examined her appearance in the bedroom mirror. The white Cleopatra tunic ended above her knees, and the gold-colored "girdle" worn over it emphasized her slim waist and the curve of her hips. Her long, wavy hair with puff bangs looked nothing like that of the Egyptian queen, except maybe in color.

The garment fit more snugly than Jillian would have liked. Bill had sworn she and his college-age sister were the same size, but Jillian knew there had to be a five- or ten-pound discrepancy. The white-and-gold sandals, however, fit perfectly.

This was the only costume they found while ransacking Kylie's closet, so she had no other choice. Jillian thought again of the dreamy expression in Bill's eyes earlier today. She'd been wearing a sweat suit then. How might he react to this? Self-consciously Jillian got out a white sweater and slipped it on.

Downstairs she found Bill waiting for her. In one hand he held the bowl of barbecued meatballs she'd made, and in the other he held a long, curved toy sabre. Jillian couldn't help but admire the way the tight purple tank top caressed the hard contours of his chest and abdomen. The shiny gold pants hugged his narrow waist, then flared into loose folds that gathered with a button at each ankle. The black, high-top athletic shoes made an interesting contrast to the turban, gold hoop earring, choker and armbands that completed the outfit.

"Are you a desert nomad or a rap musician?"

"Neither. I'm Cleopatra's bodyguard."

His gaze raked over her in a way that led Jillian to believe she'd need a bodyguard to protect her from her bodyguard. The appreciative look he sent her made her feel beautiful and desirable. And unaccountably warm. Even so, she pulled the white sweater closer together. "I don't remember Cleopatra having a bodyguard."

"She didn't need one. You do."

Mr. and Mrs. Clayton had already left to close the diner early, saying there would be few customers due to the Halloween festivities. They would meet them at the social hall. Mike had gone home to Richmond for the remainder of the weekend. Even Frank had disappeared.

Jillian remembered the time at her apartment when she'd almost lost control of the situation. It was too dangerous being alone with Bill, for she was more susceptible to his charm now than she'd been at the time of the bomb scare. As much as she had tried to prevent it from happening, Jillian was losing her heart to Bill. She'd grown accustomed to his playful pranks and good-natured teasing. And his accent no longer sounded funny to her ears. In fact, she liked the slow, gentle lilt of his deep voice.

"I guess we'd better go now," Jillian said, breaking the charged silence between them. "The party can't start without our meatballs."

Bill switched on the porch light and hung a bag of Halloween candy on the doorknob for trick-or-treaters.

"My parents tried that once," Jillian said as they walked to the car. "The first kid took all the candy, and those who came after that papered the house."

"I'm more worried about the raccoons getting it."

When they arrived at the social hall, Jillian was surprised to see people of all ages joining in the fun. Since she'd been told this was to be a square dance, she had expected mostly older attendees. Not so. Some masqueraders even brought their children along.

Besides a long table groaning under its burden of food, there were carnival-type games, face painting, and a fortune-teller at one end of the enormous room. The connecting room had been set aside for dancing or for lounging in the chairs that lined two walls. The hired musicians were still setting up their instruments. A local teen, having commandeered the microphone, produced a lively harmonica tune while a tiny witch and Frankenstein danced along.

Bill excused himself while Jillian hung her sweater in the coatroom, and he returned a few minutes later with two mugs of hot apple cider.

Handing her one, he said, "You'll be getting your recipe cards back in a day or two."

"I will? How did you manage that?"

Bill took a swallow of the cider and grinned. "I put the word out that I'll personally injure whoever took them. People around here know better than to mess with Bill Clayton," he bragged.

Jillian shot him an incredulous look as he flexed one large biceps for her benefit.

"That, plus I offered a reward for their return," he added.

"Certainly the reward is overkill," Jillian teased as she lightly pinched his arm muscle between two fingers.

His tone grew serious. "Personally I think rewarding criminal behavior is wrong, but in this case I figured it was the quickest way of getting your recipes back. Even so, once I know who stole them, I'll find a way to make them sorry they ever did it."

His implied threat made Jillian uncomfortable. She wondered what he planned to do to the culprit. Turn him or her over to the authorities? Although she believed him when he said that people knew better than to mess with Bill Clayton, she couldn't imagine him actually using physical force against anyone. No, the truth was, she didn't *want* to imagine it. Bill was a man ruled by passion. It showed in his work, in his kisses, and in his anger. She hated to think how he planned to punish the thief.

"Come on," she said, changing the subject. "I challenge you to a game of ring toss."

Before long, they had won a toy watch, a stuffed bunny and a plastic spider on a string. Jillian was so amused at his pleasure over winning that she didn't mind losing.

They strolled among clowns and devils, Bill's hand resting lightly on her back as they took in the sights and smells of the social hall.

At the fortune-teller's booth, the gypsy called out to them. "Come along, sit down, and I'll unlock the secret of your future."

Bill turned to Jillian, one eyebrow raised in question. She nodded, and they sat before "Stella, the Fortune Tella."

The diminutive woman waved her gnarled hands over a bowling ball covered with aluminum foil. Jillian could tell it was a bowling ball by the indentations of the finger holes. Stella was dressed in flowing robes and wore a garish array of makeup colors.

"Mrs. Preston?" Jillian asked.

"You child—" The old woman pointed a bony finger at Jillian. "My crystal ball tells me you should wear less black on your eyes. It makes you look cheap."

Bill snickered softly.

"But you—" Jillian began before Bill stopped her with an elbow planted firmly against her ribs.

"And you, boy," Stella said, her finger now angled at Bill. "You must speak your mind. You have something you want to say, but you're holding back." She

waved her hand again and described the image she saw
there. "Both of you are wearing something. A hat . . . a
veil . . . no, it's covering your eyes." Stella peered closer
at the bowling ball. "It looks like a mask. No, you're
both wearing blindfolds. There is something that you
are refusing to see. You must take off those blindfolds
and look at the truth."

Jillian looked at Bill to see how he was taking this
"information." He shrugged and gave her a wink.

The gesture said to humor the woman. While taping
the show with Mrs. Preston, Jillian had learned how
deeply the tiny woman and Bill cared for each other. Bill
had teased Mrs. Preston mercilessly, implying, among
other things, that she rode a motorcycle to church. And
Mrs. Preston had responded in kind, telling him to
"kiss my foot."

Stella pierced Bill with her rheumy eyes. "You're
Cleopatra's servant, aren't you?"

"I'm Abdul, her bodyguard," Bill clarified.

"That's what I said. You're afraid of telling Cleopatra what you think because she's royalty and you're
only her servant."

"Bodyguard."

"Same thing. You must stop putting her on a pedes-
tal. Now Cleo. . ." Stella turned to Jillian. "You must
never look down on Abdul, here. When you find yourself looking at his background instead of the man, you
must remember that, in bed, everyone is equal."

Chapter Eight

"My goodness, look at the time." Jillian pointed to her wristwatch. "We'd better hurry if you want to play the carnival games before the dance starts."

Thank goodness, Bill took the hint. Rising, he thanked Stella for her advice. The elderly woman's voice followed them out of the makeshift tent.

"Mark my words. Only when you take off the blindfolds will you find true happiness."

Jillian didn't stop until they were out of earshot of Stella. "I wonder if she tries to play matchmaker with everyone who goes into her tent tonight."

If Bill was embarrassed by the woman's suggestions, he didn't show it. "Probably just those who are missing what seems so obvious to her."

There was no hint of laughter in his eyes. Jillian frowned. Surely he didn't believe a fake fortune-teller's rantings.

They had shared a few kisses, but that didn't necessarily mean anything. Did it? As for that comment that everyone is equal in bed... Her cheeks heated as she recalled Stella's words. Somehow Jillian knew the saying wasn't necessarily true. She had a strong feeling that, in Bill's case, he'd be far superior to any other man.

Jerking her thoughts back to more neutral territory, she asked, "Do you want to play a game?"

Wrong question. She had been talking about the Halloween entertainment. Coming on the heels of the previous topic, the question was loaded with innuendo. Bill seemed to be mulling over the unexpected invitation.

"I mean..." Jillian glanced up, searching for the closest activity. "What's a cake walk? Do you want to do that?"

She hoped it would be a more benign experience than talking to Mrs. Preston.

As they approached the small crowd of participants, the barker announced, "This pear cake, which will go to the winner, has been donated by nineteen-year-old Belinda Harper.

Belinda stood beside the barker, smiling and holding her cake up for everyone to see.

The man continued. "Belinda says there's a very unusual ingredient in the cake. She won't tell what it is. You'll have to taste it and decide for yourself."

That was all it took to intrigue Jillian. "I have to win that cake," she told Bill.

"Well, if it isn't Boondock Bill and... Cleopatra Jill!" The announcer's booming voice caused everyone around them to turn and stare. Jillian squirmed under the intense scrutiny. Bill, on the other hand, lapped up the attention by responding with a smile and a wave. "Hoo-eee!" the man said to Jillian. "If you dressed like that on your TV show, I wouldn't miss a single episode."

Jillian automatically straightened her spine and gave a regal tilt to her chin. She refused to be cowed by some rude buffoon.

Bill took her hand in his and gave it a firm squeeze. "Are you going to start the cake walk, Ted, or are you going to stand there and yammer all night?"

At that, the man lined up the fourteen contestants and turned on the music.

"It's something like musical chairs," Bill explained. "There are thirteen sheets of paper taped to the floor. We walk around in a circle, and when the music stops, the one not standing on a paper is out. At each round, they remove a sheet until there's only one cake walker left."

They lasted through nine rounds. On the tenth, the music stopped, and Jillian raced for the white square nearest her, colliding with Bill. Off balance, she threw her arms around his waist to steady herself.

"Nope, you two can't share," the announcer said, stepping closer. He tapped Jillian on the shoulder. "You're out."

When the music started again, Jillian stood with the onlookers. Bill clenched his fist and lifted his thumb. "I'll win it for you," he said.

His intentions were apparently stronger than his luck that night, for he lasted only two more rounds.

"Well, I tried," he told Jillian as they watched the remaining two in a face-off.

She touched his arm. "Thanks anyway. Maybe Belinda will share the recipe."

A man dressed in buckskins emerged triumphant. Before Jillian had a chance to feel the sting of defeat, he had acquired a knife and was passing around slices of the coveted pear cake.

Bill raised his piece in a salute to Jillian. She tasted the cake, closing her eyes as she tried to identify the mystery ingredient.

Her eyes flew open. It was her grandmother's cake! No one else would think to balance the pears' sweet acidity with such a strange ingredient.

"This is incredible," she murmured. How could Belinda have the same recipe that had originated in her grandmother's kitchen? Her heart sank as she considered the possibility.

"What's incredible?" Bill ate his last bite of cake. "Did you figure out what's in it?"

That, and more, Jillian thought. Although she was ninety-nine-percent certain the recipe had come from the stolen collection, there was still a one-percent chance it hadn't. Jillian wouldn't voice her suspicion until she could be absolutely sure. "It's incredibly good," she said. "Would you excuse me while I ask Belinda how it's prepared?"

"Okay," Bill said, "but try not to talk shop all night."

Jillian watched as he wandered over to one of the booths and sat down. She recalled his menacing threat to make the guilty party sorry. If Belinda was guilty, Jillian wondered, would he cause her to lose her job at his parents' diner?

The young woman's livelihood could depend on how Jillian handled the situation.

She weaved her way through a small throng of party-goers. "Belinda, the cake was delicious."

The girl turned. "Thank you, I made it my—" When she realized who had complimented her, dread glimmered briefly in her eyes. "I made it myself," she said after recovering her composure.

"Mashed black-eyed peas to cut the sugar and tartness. My grandmother used to do the very same thing."

"As a matter of fact," Belinda confessed, "I got the recipe from your show. You made it look so good, I just had to try it."

She sounded overly perky. Jillian gritted her teeth in frustration. She had as much as caught the girl redhanded. That recipe had never been demonstrated on "Cooking With Jillian."

"I'm so glad you enjoyed it." Jillian's voice sounded more even than she felt inside.

"Oh, I love all your recipes," Belinda chattered on. "I was wondering about your lamb duchesse . . . since I don't have a pastry bag, can I just plop the mashed potatoes around the edges with a spoon?"

Jillian answered the question and discussed some cooking techniques with Belinda, trying to stall while she decided on the best course of action.

The lamb duchesse, as well as the pear cake, had never been demonstrated on her show. In fact, those were two of many recipes she had been saving for firsttime use in a cookbook.

Her first inclination was to confront the girl and demand she return the cards. The drawback, however, was that since Belinda had already lied twice about seeing the recipes on her show, she could just as easily lie and say she never took the recipe cards.

The other option was to tell Bill, in which case Belinda would most likely be fired and Jillian might never see her collection again.

Bill returned, grinning for all he was worth. Or, as he would put it, "like a mule eating briars." Jillian smiled. He certainly had a way with words.

"Aw, cool!" said Belinda. "You got a tattoo. Oh, there's Eric. Gotta go."

In a flash, she was gone, leaving Jillian with her third and final option. Do nothing. Maybe it was for the best. A Halloween party wasn't exactly the place to handle such a delicate situation.

Her gaze fell on Bill's muscular upper arm. An image of a cat curled into a cozy ball had been produced with amazing detail. It even had black-tipped ears, nose and feet.

"Why did you get a tattoo of a Siamese cat on your arm?"

"I was too ticklish to let him put it on my chest."

Jillian sighed. She'd never met anyone as impulsive as Bill Clayton. A tattoo. Ugh! She wondered if he really considered it macho to have a picture on his arm. And if he did, why did he choose a picture of a cute cat?

"Don't you like it?"

If he thought it was attractive, she wouldn't burst his bubble. Besides, it was already done. "The artwork is quite good," she admitted with complete honesty.

Bill beamed with pleasure. Somehow, that one gesture was enough to make her reconsider how her feelings had grown for him lately. It wasn't just the tattoo— she'd seen plenty of them on the Army recruits. It was his attitude about it. And about a lot of other things.

The tattoo was enough to remind Jillian, with shocking clarity, just how different their worlds really were.

"The music's starting. Come on. I'll teach you to square-dance." Bill led her to the dance floor where they squared off with three other couples.

Before long, Jillian forgot about the tattoo as they do-si-do'd and sashayed with the rest of the dancers. It was fun watching Bill enjoy it with such gusto, and Jillian loved the exhilarating way it made her heart race. And, as much as she tried to deny it, she loved the way Bill caught her about the waist and swung her before passing her off to her next partner.

Laughing and breathless, they left the social hall just before midnight. Jillian hated for the evening to end.

As they drove along the dark, winding roads, Jillian realized tonight was the first time she'd had so much fun since, well . . . she couldn't remember ever having such a wonderful time.

But why did it have to be with Bill Clayton, of all people? Why couldn't they just like each other well enough to work happily together? Why couldn't she have had this exuberantly enjoyable evening with a college professor, or a suit-clad businessman or a nice, predictable accountant?

The answers seemed to seep up from her subconscious. Because A—the college professor and businessman, suitable as they might be, just weren't Bill Clayton, and B—the predictable accountant would never have taken her to a square dance in the first place.

They came upon a scenic overlook, and Bill pulled off and parked the car. "Come on, I want to show you where I used to go when I was a kid."

When he *was* a kid? Jillian almost laughed, thinking that description could be applied in the present tense. She got out and followed him to a narrow path that led to a boulder jutting out over a steep precipice. An ancient, almost bare tree reached over the hideaway, providing a spidery canopy overhead. Another, narrower rock formation created a shelf below the first, reminding Jillian of a footrest on a beautician's chair.

She took his outstretched hand and tentatively stepped down off the dirt path. "Are you sure this is safe?"

"Solid as a rock," Bill assured her. "People have been coming to Lookout Rock for centuries. What a view," he said, sweeping a hand over the valley below them.

What a view, indeed. Jillian sat beside Bill on a soft, mossy area. Lights, some clustered together and others scattered about the valley, winked up at them. Their glittering presence created a mystical accompaniment to the moon and stars that strove to outshine them.

"See those headlights over there?" Bill said, leaning close and pointing to the left, past Jillian. "Look down and to the right. That orange and blue light is the sign on my parents' diner." He seemed proud, almost possessive of the sights he offered her.

Jillian tossed a pebble over the edge. Several seconds passed before she heard it hit, then tumble through the underbrush. "Lookout Rock, Lookout Point, Lookout Hill—there must be at least one in every state."

"Ah, but not all of them have nicknames," Bill countered. "To the teenagers, this one is known as Make-out Rock."

"Is that why you brought me here?"

"No, but we can always change the agenda. And then we could put our initials here with the rest."

For one insane minute, Jillian gave in to the fantasy of his suggested agenda. Would he be rough and demanding, or slow and sensual? Either way, the image of

the two of them entwined together was enough to draw
pangs of longing from deep inside her. She shuddered
with a need that transcended any she'd ever experienced before.

"Cold?" Bill slipped an arm around her, allowing his
thumb to stroke her cheek in idle play.

Jillian turned away from it, trying to escape the drug-
inducing effects of his touch, and found Bill gazing
down at her. He looked serious. Not at all like the rap-
scallion, Boondock Bill. His steady intensity unsettled
her.

"Is something wrong?" she asked.

He allowed a long silence before answering. "Yes. It's
been over a week, and you still haven't paid off your
debt to me."

"I don't understand. I never borrowed any money
from you."

"That last biscuit was rightfully mine. You owe me a
kiss."

"As I remember it, Frank won fair and square. *He*
kissed me, remember?"

"A lick on the hand doesn't qualify as a kiss. Let me
show you how it should have been done." Bill's hand
slid to her neck, exerting gentle pressure to bring her
closer. The other hand settled on her waist.

Jillian closed her eyes and pressed her lips for the inevitable kiss. A simple little peck should pay off whatever "debt" he felt she owed him. And satisfy this crazy
need to feel his lips on hers. Maybe.

His mouth touched hers, gently at first, then with a
warm kneading that loosened her stiff pucker. After a
slow pass over her lips, his tongue parted the tender
flesh, at first invading, them stimulating Jillian's senses
until she grew shaky with desire.

Mindlessly she responded in kind, savoring the delectable way he tasted. He leaned back on one elbow and started drawing careless circles on her side. Pushing the white sweater aside, his hand found the swelling of her breast. Jillian's arms went up around his neck, allowing him freer access to create those pleasure-inducing designs on her body.

Bill pushed her back against the moss, his lips tracing insistently down her neck and along her collarbone to the sensitive shallow where the two ridges met. Then his forays plunged lower while Jillian's fingers wound themselves into his thick hair. In a moment, the white fabric was pushed aside and one pink-tipped breast lay bare to the cool night air, and to his hungering lips.

Jillian felt her nipples harden and a tingling sensation begin at the core of her femininity as he exposed the other breast to his plundering lips.

She lay back, opening herself to his inquisitive exploration, silently begging him to fill her, to fill the need he had planted inside her soul and her body.

She pulled him to her, arching against him, her hands roaming the broad expanse of his chest. She pushed the tight-fitting muscle shirt up and delighted when the short, soft hair rubbed across her sensitized nipples.

Her hands traced the hard planes of his back beneath the denim jacket, as Bill shifted his weight over her. All the while, his lips and teeth wrought sweet torture on her mouth, her eyelids, her ears, and her neck.

"Mmm, Jillian, I need you," he breathed. "Let me love you."

"Please." It was more a whimper than a word. More a plea than a reply.

A slight stirring of air dried the moisture on her brow and raised gooseflesh from scalp to toe. Or maybe it was caused by her reaction to the knowledge that she had driven him to such a level of excitement.

Jillian cried out, wanting him more than she'd wanted anything or anyone ever before. Bill claimed her lips again, this time sucking hungrily.

His breath puffed raggedly against her neck. He abruptly rolled off and gathered her close, her head resting on his arm. The sudden change in his manner startled her. She had wanted him to take her to the heights of passion—to release the frustration that had been steadily building within her over the past few weeks. And now he had ceased the sweet torture that he had started in her soul.

Bill toyed with her hair. If not for the uncomfortable hardness of the rock under them, Jillian could have lain this way forever. He lay on his side gazing down at her with a softness in his expression she could not read. No matter what it meant, she liked having him look at her that way.

"What an evening," she said quietly.

Bill scowled and lay back beside her.

"I'm sorry," he said. "I didn't mean for this to happen."

His words hit her like a slap. Sorry? She was the one who should be sorry, almost abandoning her well-founded belief that they could never be more than friends. And for what? One episode of impulsive pleasure. Glorious, mind-reeling pleasure.

No matter how good it had been, she still had to work with him. How would this affect their working relationship?

"No," she said. "I should have been the one to stop it." She was the sensible one. She should have had the presence of mind to see that Bill was merely following a physical impulse. It was little different than his other spontaneous outbursts in life. What she couldn't figure was why he had stopped when she had been so willing.

"I wasn't talking about making love," he said. "I want it to happen." His voice rumbled against her temple. "But, although I'm often spontaneous, I'm not usually stupid."

It was bad enough that she'd been rejected like an overeager teenager. Now he was cutting her to the quick by saying how foolish he was for almost bedding her. "No," she said, starting to rise. "The stupidity is all mine."

Bill caught her arm and pulled her back to him. "That's not what I meant." He drew a slow breath before continuing. "It's been a long time since I've been serious about anyone. I don't carry protection around with me as a matter of course."

For a moment, Jillian stopped breathing. *Serious about anyone.* She considered the possibility that he had actually fallen in love with her. She knew she cared for him, but was it love? She didn't know. All she knew was that, around Bill Clayton, it was difficult to think straight, much less consider the ultimate consequences of her actions.

Jillian tensed as his words about protection sank in and drove home just how foolhardy her actions had been. She had stopped taking the pill after her divorce, yet she'd been so caught up in the moment that she hadn't given a fleeting thought to birth control. And, with a pregnancy, her career goals could have gone right down the tubes or, at the least, been stalled for many more years.

A gust of night air blew around them, prompting Jillian to pull her sweater closer around herself. "I'm not usually so flighty," she admitted. "So I'm glad you showed some restraint for a change."

Bill laughed. "Thank you, I think. But it was just barely." He touched her shoulder and followed the line of her neck to the point of her chin. "You're a beautiful woman, Jillian Reed. I find it very hard to exercise self-control around you."

His words were true. Until this evening, he had shown little restraint about anything. Jillian wondered how their near lack of control tonight would impact their working relationship on the show. Would he become more unruly on the set? Would she blush and become speechless if he made a loaded remark? The answer to both was: most likely.

She couldn't let this happen. She couldn't let one night of indiscretion ruin her chances for success. The teasing and joking she had come to expect, and even participate in, had made the taping sessions more fun. But she couldn't lose sight of her professionalism.

His fingers roamed up her neck and found an earlobe, then moved to explore the curved crevices. She tried to remember why she had set such an ambitious goal in the first place, but Bill's exhilirating caresses clouded her thinking. When she finally remembered, it seemed rather silly that she had been working so hard in order to prove to someone, who was no longer in her life, that she was *not* inept.

For the first time, Quint's taunts and put-downs didn't matter anymore. Nor did it matter whether her show became syndicated. She would be thrilled if it was but, with or without syndication, her show was a success. She had proven to *herself* that she could overcome obstacles such as stage fright and still do a good job.

She had succeeded, and there were still a few months left until her thirtieth birthday.

She was happy to be able to separate Quint from her professional goals. But could she separate him from her personal relationships, too? Would the hurt she had suffered at her ex-husband's hands continue to dictate how she responded to Bill? Or any other man, for that matter? Until she knew for sure that she was free of Quint, it would be wiser and kinder not to enter a relationship with Bill. Why should he have to suffer because of her unresolved problems?

For now, perhaps it would be best to delay their getting involved. If she claimed it was for the sake of the show, perhaps he wouldn't press too hard. She gave him a tentative smile.

She took his hand in hers, effectively stilling the crazy sensations he was producing in her.

"Bill, it flatters me to know that you find me attractive. I . . . find you attractive, too," she admitted.

His thumb traced an erotic path over the palm of her hand and up to her wrist. He wasn't making this any easier.

"However, I think it's a mistake to let any impulsive actions of ours get in the way of our work."

"Don't worry, I won't kiss you on the set. On the lips maybe, but we can save that for afterward."

Even in the pale moonlight, she could see him grinning.

"That won't work, either," she said wryly. "Our viewers are already asking if we're engaged, and we've only just discovered for ourselves that we're attracted to each other. What will they think if we actually do follow through on this . . . new awareness?"

"Who cares what they think?"

"I do. And you should, too, since our performance and ratings will ultimately affect your station."

Bill crossed his arms over his knees. "So what are you suggesting?"

"I'm suggesting that we act with more professionalism if we don't want the ratings to suffer. We should just forget about this attraction thing between us and concentrate on our work."

Chapter Nine

"Forget about it? Just like that?" He snapped his fingers for emphasis.

"My priority is to make the show a success. I thought it was yours, too."

"It is, but it's not my only priority. Jillian, I am not Boondock Bill. The man you almost made love with tonight is a totally separate person. Bill Clayton wants more than work and high ratings."

"But Bill Clayton's feelings affect Boondock Bill's performance," she argued, "the same as Jillian Reed's feelings affect the Cooking Lady's concentration on the show. It's for this reason I think we should keep things professional, both on and off the set. Maybe, if we still feel this way in two or three years, after we're more established, we can decide to take things further."

Maybe by then, she thought, *I'll have put to rest my ghosts from the past.*

Bill slowly shook his head. "You astound me. You talk about romance as if it's something you can put on hold, or *decide* about. Tell me, what made you *decide* to marry the man who's now your ex-husband?"

"Quint?"

"Is there more than one?"

"No, of course not." Jillian stared back at Bill, trying to read the expression on his face. "He was attentive, and polite. We came from similar backgrounds. And I had thought that we would complement each other, both professionally and socially."

"Sounds more like a merger than a marriage."

"I beg your—"

"What about passion? Did you ever have moments when you couldn't keep your hands off each other?"

"I really don't think that's any of your business."

"It is if you're trying to handle our relationship the way you handled your marriage."

Jillian grew silent. She had made a mistake with Quint. She certainly didn't want to repeat those mistakes with Bill.

"I'm waiting."

"Quint was a handsome man. The physical part of our marriage wasn't unpleasant."

"That's not what I asked you." Bill considered the answer she had given him. It told him all he needed to know. He knew that, deep down, a passion burned inside Jillian Reed. He wanted to be the one to unleash it, show her the power of it. But she was too bent on ruling her life with logic to see what she was missing.

Intuitively Bill knew the chemistry between them was part of what kept viewers watching from day to day. Mrs. Preston had even compared them to the characters of the "Moonlighting" TV show. And although the elderly woman bragged of having changed his diapers when he was a baby, Bill knew his eccentric neighbor tuned in for more reasons than that she liked him and his humor. As Stella, she had advised him to do exactly what he'd been trying to work up courage to do for the past few weeks: tell Jillian his true feelings.

But now was not the time. Her mind and her heart were closed. Locked tight. No, tonight his words of love would fall on deaf ears. Maybe later he'd find the key that would unlock her heart. Until then he'd have to play by her rules of logic.

"Have it your way," he said. "Henceforth, we are now business associates. Co-workers. Employer and employee." Bill clutched his heart, made a plucking motion, and put it in an imaginary spot in the night air. "There. My feelings are now on a shelf. You are safe with me." He went one step further. "Consider me your brother."

Jillian shook his hand. "It's a deal . . . Bubba."

"Bubba's my cousin."

"Billy Bob?"

"That's my uncle." Bill couldn't help smiling at her teasing jibes. If he'd brought her this far, maybe he could overcome her other barriers as well. "C'mon, sis, my buns are getting numb sitting on this rock. Let's go home."

They stood, and Jillian took care to fix her disarray. She smoothed her hair and adjusted her dress. As they reached the car, another vehicle pulled in, sweeping its headlights over both of them. Bits of leaves clung to her hair, green moss stains showed on the elbow of her sweater, and the decorative gold belt hung at an odd angle on her hips.

"You look ravished," Bill told her.

A teenage couple got out and walked past them down the path to the rock. They giggled, and the girl's voice carried back to them.

"What are those old people doing here?"

The next week passed quickly. The tattoo on Bill's arm faded after a couple of days. Bill claimed that the cat had been intended as Cleopatra's pet and that it had disappeared due to a lack of cuddling. Fortunately this was said in a private joke instead of in front of the camera. Other than that, his behavior was quite brotherly.

Like a brother, he took great glee in proving her wrong about her Canine Crunchies. They filmed the cook-off in the Claytons' kitchen where Frank turned his nose up at Jillian's gourmet dog treats and, much to Bill's delight, chose the steak trimmings instead.

The evening before they were to return home to Richmond, Bill drove Jillian to the diner for an ice-cream sundae. After they placed their orders, Jillian excused herself. She found Belinda straightening the candy display near the cash register.

"Have you tried any more of my recipes lately?" Jillian asked casually.

Belinda faltered, then resumed her work, never looking directly at Jillian. "Yeah, some. I've gotten some good recipes off your show."

"That's interesting," said Jillian, "because the pear cake and lamb duchesse were never demonstrated on the show."

"Oh."

"I'll be leaving tomorrow, Belinda. I must have those recipes back. All of them," she stressed. "If you do as

I ask, then this whole incident can stay between you and me.''

The girl straightened and faced Jillian. "It's not like you think. I didn't steal your recipes,'' she said. "I only borrowed them. I was going to give the cards back after I copied down the ones that looked good.''

Jillian frowned, trying to make sense of what she was hearing. "Why?''

"I've been working here for almost three years—full-time since I finished high school. Yet, here I am, still sweeping floors and washing dishes. I'm ready for a promotion.'' Her eyes begged Jillian for understanding. "I wanted to prove to Mr. and Mrs. Clayton that I can handle the cooking.''

Though their goals were different, Jillian saw that Belinda's drive to advance in the restaurant was as strong as her own desire had been to succeed with her television show. "Taking something without asking permission only proves that you can't be trusted,'' she said gently.

Belinda looked past her, dread shadowing her face.

A large, masculine hand touched Jillian's shoulder. "What's taking you so long?'' asked Bill. "Our sundaes are ready.''

The teenager looked as if she were expecting the worst.

"Oh, look, they're all out of wintergreen,'' Jillian said, reaching for a pack of candy. "Spearmint will do for now, but I'll stop in tomorrow and pick up the other,'' she said to Belinda, adding a significant wink.

The girl flashed her a nervous smile, then quickly returned to the candy display. Bill raised an eyebrow at her curious behavior but said nothing until they were seated and well into their sundaes.

"What time were you planning on stopping by to pick up the recipe cards?" At Jillian's startled expression, he smoothly added, "I mean, your, uh, wintergreen mints."

"You knew?"

"She was the only one besides my parents and me who had easy access to the office. Any customer going in there would have been immediately noticed." Like a child, he stirred his ice cream until it looked like pudding. "Plus, I saw her jamming something into her purse and forcing it closed the day before you noticed them missing."

Jillian dropped her spoon into her dish. "Why didn't you tell me? Or better yet, why didn't you confront Belinda? I've been a wreck for two weeks, thinking I'd never see my collection again." She felt like kicking him under the table for allowing her to worry needlessly.

Bill leaned back in the booth and stretched his arms across the back of his seat. Jillian tried to ignore how his pullover sweater stretched becomingly across his chest.

"I didn't know for sure what was in the purse. Belinda's basically an honest person. I figured if she was given a chance she'd come clean on her own."

"And if she didn't?"

"I would have asked Mom and Dad to let her go."

Jillian knew instnctively that he would have done so without a second's hesitation. He was as honest as the day was long, and he expected the same from everyone else. Once again, guilt prickled Jillian's conscience at how she had, even if only briefly, thought he might take the cards in an attempt to bend her to his will. She winced inwardly as she remembered giving Belinda the benefit of the doubt until she was one-hundred-percent certain the teenager was the true culprit.

She couldn't blame him for her own reactions. Logic had little to do with her actions since Bill Clayton had come into her life. Things that had once seemed so sensible and orderly now looked tame and boring.

Her priorities were all jumbled up. Just a few months ago, when she had interviewed with Memphis Reason for the position at WXYZ, her single-minded goal had been to make her name a household word by the time she reached her thirtieth birthday. Now, sitting in a truck-stop diner in southwest Virginia as she enjoyed the company of a magnificent mountain man whose mere voice had once annoyed her, she was surprised to discover that her goal was no longer so terribly important. In retrospect, it became clear that her desire to make a juvenile prediction come true had started with a classmate's taunt at her high school reunion. Her goal was unrealistic but, worse than that, it wasn't true to herself. Her self-confidence had been shattered by Quint's philandering ways, and her impulsive statement at the reunion had been a misguided effort to prove her worth, even if only to people she hadn't cared enough about to keep in touch with for ten years. And when Quint had joined the group in their laughter, she had wanted more than ever to prove him wrong.

Now, however, she knew it didn't matter what Quint or her graduating class thought of her. Or even Bill, for that matter. The important thing was to be true to herself.

A couple of months ago she wouldn't have believed it possible, but now she actually liked her life: the small suburb outside of Richmond that was now her home, cooking for the homeless once a week, and most of all her time with Bill, both on the set and off.

Yes, if anyone was true to himself, it was Bill Clayton. He'd never pretended to be anything other than what he was. He was comfortable enough with his own identity to take the nickname Boondock Bill and poke fun at himself. Jillian thought of Cooter, the old man at the soup kitchen who wanted to believe he was a chef, or doctor, or anyone other than himself.

Cooter did so because he had a mental or emotional problem. But hadn't Jillian done the same, pretending to be a cool sophisticate when, inside, she was a quivering mass of jelly? The only excuse she could offer was that the act created a wall behind which no one—not even herself—could see how scared she really was.

She looked up to find Bill watching her, his greenish-gray eyes fixed dreamily upon her and his lip quirked slightly upward on one side. "You were so deep in thought, I figured I might have to throw you a rope."

"Just doing a little introspection," she admitted.

"Find anything interesting?"

"Interesting, maybe, but not very pretty."

"I find that hard to believe."

Jillian studied the man who made her life both heaven and hell these past few weeks. Not long ago, she would have been bothered by his shaggy hair and holey jeans and maybe even the little diner in which they sat. Now . . . well, now she saw these as evidence of who Bill was and where he came from. And she liked them because they were his.

She liked the way his hair curled slightly at the neck because it was too long. She liked the deep timbre of his voice and the way he left the *g* dangling on words like "nothin'" and "puddin'." She even liked the town and people of Fullerton, not only because they were wonderful in their own right, but because they offered her a peek at who and what had shaped the man she had come to love.

Love! Her first reaction was to deny the thought, to pretend she had really been thinking of the respect and admiration she felt for Bill.

A tiny voice in the back of her mind nudged her, reminding Jillian of her resolve to be true to herself. Slowly, tentatively, she acknowledged that she did, indeed, love Bill Clayton.

Now that she recognized it for what it was, things were beginning to make sense. It explained why he got under her skin, right from the start, and why she had reacted so strongly to him. It also explained why she had thrown caution to the wind on Lookout Rock last weekend. There had been more involved than hormones and a starry night.

Looking back, Jillian realized she had been in love with Bill for quite some time but had been too busy hiding behind her wall of defensiveness to recognize it. It was possible she had started loving him after their first meeting but had been too blind—and conceited— to see it.

How things had changed! Now she wondered if she was good enough for Bill. She wasn't sure.

"Looks like you need cleats and a rappeling rope to come back this time."

Jillian blinked and cleared her throat. Picking up her spoon, she stirred her melted ice cream. "I'm sorry. I haven't been very good company this evening."

"Care to share your innermost thoughts with your dear ol' brother?"

If she didn't know better, she would have guessed he had read her mind and was mocking her. She shook her head. No way would she let him know what she'd been thinking. Not now. Not after demanding they keep things platonic for the next two or three years until their careers were established.

Two or three years! She doubted she'd last two or three days.

Why had he ever kissed her? Or touched her? Or even looked at her with those incredibly knowing eyes? Now she knew what she'd been missing, and that knowledge would torment her until they stopped the brother-sister act.

A crease appeared between his thick eyebrows. "You've been working hard these past two weeks." He stood and held out his hand to her. "Let's go home and go to bed."

Jillian's eyes widened. The image conjured up by his suggestion was not what she should be thinking about in her present state of mind.

On their way out, they called good-night to his father. During the short drive back to the house, Jillian decided what she must do.

She would prove to Bill, and to herself, that she could throw off her overly proper ways. No longer would she silently or openly plead with Bill to control his spontaneous outbursts. After all, what harm did he do? At the least, his playfulness had helped her learn to relax and enjoy the moment. Who could tell? Maybe she'd drop her poise and surprise everyone by joining in the fun more often.

Jillian smiled as they entered the house and walked up the stairs together. She wondered how Bill would respond to her unexpected turnabout.

They stopped at her bedroom door. Bill gazed down at her, his eyes appearing black in the dimly lighted hall. "G'night, Jillian."

She lifted her face to him and closed her eyes. He planted a dry, brotherly kiss on her forehead.

When she opened her eyes, she saw that he was smiling. It was a teasing, mocking smile. "Sleep tight, sis."

Then he turned and disappeared into the room he had shared with Mike. Reluctantly Jillian went into her bedroom feeling lonelier than she had ever felt in her entire lifetime. With the frequent moves demanded by her father's Army career, she had made few close friends during her childhood. Each time they had uprooted, her heart had felt so empty. But those experiences were nothing compared to sleeping alone in Bill's bed.

She dressed quickly and huddled under the heavy quilt. She tossed and turned, unable to get comfortable, her mind producing images like a slide show. Most of the pictures were of Bill.

Why did she have to discover she loved him *after* she'd made him promise to keep things businesslike between them? What an idiot she was, squirming in his bed when she really wanted to—

No, that wouldn't be proper.

But the thought kept poking at her, prodding her to take action. After all, hadn't she decided to be more spontaneous? To throw off her proper ways?

A wicked grin crossed her face as she imagined Bill's reaction. And if she felt like a fool for doing it, the feeling wouldn't last forever. In the morning, she could explain away her foolishness by claiming to have been sleepwalking.

Jillian got up, not bothering to put on her robe. She couldn't help wondering if she was the only person to plan a spontaneous act.

The floor creaked beneath her feet. She froze in that spot before working up the courage to open the door to the adjoining bathroom. Not bothering to turn on the light, she pushed the door open to the next room. She paused, letting her eyes adjust to the darkness, and tried to get her bearings in the unfamiliar room.

To her right was a dresser with a small television on it. A pair of twin beds jutted from the opposite wall, reminding Jillian that Bill had been sharing his sister's room with Mike.

With a small gasp, Jillian turned to flee back to the safety of her own room. Then she remembered the cameraman had gone home after their last taping today.

She took a deep gulp of air and clutched her racing heart. Approaching the bed with the large lump in it, she looked down at the sleeping figure. His face was relaxed, giving him a deceptively angelic appearance. He lay on his side, his top arm flung over the edge of the mattress. Jillian knelt down on the rug beside the bed and leaned toward him.

Without opening his eyes, he said, "If you're after the candy under my bed, you can forget it."

Jillian jerked, smothering a scream behind her hand.

Bill rose up on one elbow and peered at her through the dark veil of night.

"You're awake," Jillian managed to say.

"I am now."

"Why did you think I wanted your candy?" It was a stupid question, but it kept him from asking her the obvious one: Why was she in his room?

"Kylie used to sneak into my room and swipe my secret stash. If that's what sisters do, I figured you were after the same."

"Not exactly." She paused, trying to think whether to tell him what she was spontaneously doing, or just do it.

He sat up in bed and propped the pillow behind him. Then he patted the blanket, inviting her to sit beside him.

She perched on the edge, facing him. "Don't you get cold sleeping without a T-shirt?" She didn't dare speculate whether he was wearing anything else.

"I'm very warm-blooded." Because of the huskiness of his voice, it sounded more like an offer to prove it than a statement of fact. "So...you came in here to offer fashion advice on my nightwear?"

"No." It was too late to change her mind now. May as well go through with it. She wondered if she could still use the sleepwalking defense. "You kissed me good night earlier. But I didn't kiss *you.*"

He looked at her warily.

"It seemed only fair," she added lamely.

Bill shrugged. Leaning forward, he turned his cheek toward her.

She prepared to kiss him on the cheek, wishing all the while that she had the nerve to draw him to her and give him a long, most unsisterly kiss.

It was as if Bill had been wishing for the same, for he turned slightly so that her lips would meet his. They both responded with much more than a brotherly-sisterly peck, and Jillian didn't mind one bit.

After a second's hesitation, Bill's hands went around her, skimming the dip of her waist, then settling higher, just under the curve of her breasts.

Jillian liked the feel of his touch, but she knew she was courting trouble. In a man's bedroom, at night, wearing nothing but a flimsy nightgown...trouble with a capital *T.* It was the kind of trouble she looked forward to investigating soon, but not tonight. Despite her newfound sense of spontaneity, her common sense won out.

His mouth was warm and welcoming. Jillian hated to end the kiss. With a gentle nip of his lower lip, she reluctantly drew back and moved toward the door. "Good night," she whispered, her voice low and sensual. "Don't let the bed bugs bite."

An hour later, when she finally drifted off to a fitful sleep, she could still see the look of raw, hungering need on Bill's face. That look had mirrored her own feelings.

The next day, Bill didn't say anything about her midnight visit, but he seemed to be watching her with an interest more intense than he had shown previously.

They retrieved the recipe cards that had suddenly been found in an obscure corner of the diner's office, and bade their farewells to Bill's parents and neighbors.

Though she'd only known them a short time, Jillian would miss the Claytons, Mrs. Preston and the rest of her new friends. Even Belinda.

Two weeks ago she'd been against the idea of coming to Fullerton. Now she wouldn't trade the experience for anything. She was looking at the world through different eyes, and she liked the new perspective.

Back home, her new attitude spilled over to everyone who came in contact with her. Jillian enjoyed the look of surprise on the receptionist's face when she bubbled an enthusiastic "Good morning!" instead of making her usual quiet entrance. She was beginning to see the thrill Bill got out of shocking people with his offbeat sense of humor.

"Well, uh, good morning to you, too," the receptionist returned. She handed Jillian a stack of envelopes and notes. "While you were gone, a certified letter came for you from a cooking institute in D.C., and a Chef Verni has called at least twice."

Jillian turned the official-looking envelope over in her hand. Why would her alma mater, a prestigious cooking school in Washington, be contacting her? She remembered Chef Verni as the head chef and from writeups in the trade journals she subscribed to.

She thanked the receptionist and wandered back to her office where she could absorb the information in private. With trembling fingers, she unsealed the envelope and unfolded the crisp beige stationery. She scanned it quickly, bypassing the introduction and focusing on the main thrust of the letter.

...accept our invitation to join our staff... contact us by November 19 to arrange to meet and tour the facility.

A job offer! And at the nation's best cooking school, no less. Jillian sat down as she took in the enormity of it. Competition among students to attend the school was so stiff, Jillian might not have been accepted if not for her sheer persistence. After being turned down the first time, she had contacted her former home-economics instructors from the various junior high and high schools she'd attended, as well as the Army chefs who'd known her and everyone she'd ever catered a party for, and deluged the institute with letters of recommendation. Only then had the board accepted her application.

And now they were *inviting* her to join the faculty. She supposed Chef Verni had called to try to influence her decision.

Jillian laid the letter on her desk. The chair's hinges squeaked in protest as she stretched back and laced her fingers behind her neck.

What timing. If she'd received the letter sooner, she might not have given it serious consideration since she'd been so intent on achieving her goal with her cooking show. The offer tempted her—she had no contract with WXYZ, and to list a position with the institute on her résumé would be quite impressive. Plus, she had always loved teaching. But she also loved her job as host of "Cooking With Jillian." Now—now she was only confused.

Maybe she should call Chef Verni to hear him out. She was reaching for the phone when Bill popped in.

"We need you in the studio in ten minutes." He balanced on one foot, half in and half out of her office, where he grasped the doorjamb. "What's the matter? Is something wrong?"

She had never been very good at masking her feelings, which was why she had practiced so hard at it all her life. And now, on this new footing with Bill, she was sure he could read her like a grade-school primer.

Bill entered. He moved a chair from the front of her desk, turning it around to straddle it backward beside her. Jillian noted that he had never sat across from her, usually preferring to prowl the room or perch on the corner of her desk or two-drawer filing cabinet.

"Nothing's wrong," she assured him after a moment of hesitation, but she could tell he didn't fully believe her. "I got a job offer."

Bill's reaction was guarded.

Now that she no longer felt the need to prove her worth through her television show, she supposed she *could* consider this opportunity seriously. Her head said she shouldn't take the offer lightly. But her heart told her to stay with the man she loved.

"Is it another TV station?"

Jillian brought her hands from behind her head and started toying with the letter. "No. The offer came from a well-known cooking institute in Washington. They want an answer in ten days."

"What are you going to tell them?"

Oh, Bill, she wanted to blurt out, *if I knew you loved me as much as I love you, I'd reject them flat.* But what if she sacrificed this once-in-a-lifetime chance, only to discover later that his interest in her was only fleeting? That was a risk she wasn't willing to take.

"I'm not sure," she said.

Chapter Ten

Jillian promised Bill she wouldn't decide on the job offer until the tenth day. Postponing served her purpose as well since she would rather not even think about it yet, not until she learned Bill's true feelings.

She did, however, call Chef Verni, who was quite persuasive. He had several exciting teaching projects in mind. The idea of going back into the classroom lured her even though she now felt comfortable doing the "Cooking With Jillian" show and actually preferred it to the job prospect in Washington. But she wanted to make sure her decision was based on a planned career strategy rather than the simple fact that she liked her current job or that she didn't want to part from Bill. Even so, she still needed to know where she stood with him.

Jillian peered over his shoulder as he stirred the simmering spaghetti sauce. "The noodles should be ready soon," she prompted.

"I'll check." He lifted a strand from the bubbling water and started to taste the pasta.

"That's not how you test for doneness." Jillian picked up the noodle with her fingers and hurled it at the kitchen cabinet. The camera followed the flying noodle to the cabinet door, where it now adhered in loopy curves.

Bill turned and stared at her, puzzlement creasing his forehead in a vertical line.

"Done." Jillian smiled. "See? It sticks."

It wasn't as funny as it would have been if Bill had done it, but she was new at this spontaneity thing. Her sense of comedic timing could use some work, but it was a start. And it felt good.

Jillian was delighted that he seemed taken aback by her uncharacteristic playfulness, even though she'd been pulling such stunts all week.

First, there had been the episode she'd secretly planned with the sound-effects man. It had been difficult keeping a straight face when she had assigned Bill the task of slicing hot dogs for a casserole. His startled expression had been priceless when the sound of a dog's prerecorded yips filled the set with each stroke of his knife.

Then she had placed a mechanical hand in a pot of soup, setting the prop to rise up out of the liquid just as Bill was about to stir it.

It had been fun planning these gags, and she looked forward to more.

She rather liked turning the tables on Bill for a change. A momentary shadow passed over her heart as she thought how such behavior would be frowned upon at the institute.

Bill stared at the noodle on the cabinet door. "Where'd you learn that trick?"

"Every self-respecting cook knows that spaghetti is done when it sticks to the ceiling. There are too many lights up there," she said, pointing above them, "so I had to make do."

Gradually realization dawned on Bill that Jillian was having a great time surprising him with his own brand of humor. It was hard to believe this was the cool, reserved Miss Reed who had once asked him to tone down his funning around on the set.

Bill grinned and nodded at the studio hand. While Jillian finished dishing out the spaghetti, the off-camera assistant set up a large fan at the end of the counter and turned it on its highest setting.

The wind whipped around them, tossing Jillian's hair. Bill was so fascinated watching her long brown locks fly like the mane of a wild horse that he almost missed the white object blowing past him on the counter.

"Oh, look," he said, grabbing the envelope, "here's some fan mail."

Holding her hair to keep it out of her face, she suppressed a grin and rolled her eyes. She strongly suspected he was trying to top her stunts. The assistant abruptly turned off the fan and moved it away from the set.

Jillian pulled her hair back and refastened it with the large barrette. Bill handed her the envelope. "It's for you."

She held it for a moment, wondering what kind of mischief he was up to this time.

"Read it to us," he urged.

Anyone with an expression that angelic had to be up to some sort of devilishness.

Carefully she unfolded the letter, half expecting something to pop out at her. There was only a short poem, which she scanned before reading aloud.

"Roses are red.
The stems are green.
Your show's the best
That I've ever seen."

It was signed "B.C." Jillian smiled at Bill. "That's very sweet," she said. "Maybe we could invite Mr. or Ms. B.C. to join us on the show."

Bill hesitated. "Maybe we shouldn't put our viewer on the spot."

"Then let's open the invitation to the rest of our fans."

Bill did an exaggerated double-take, then pressed his palm to Jillian's forehead as if feeling for a fever.

"It worked out better than I expected when we were in Fullerton. I thought it would be fun to continue having guests once or twice a week."

At that, Bill pressed his palm to his own forehead.

They finished the show by inviting people to send their favorite recipes in order to be chosen as a guest. Afterward Jillian retreated to her office. She needed some quiet time to think. Today was Thursday, which meant she had a week in which to make up her mind about the job offer.

She lifted a slip of paper out of her chair. Sitting down, she unfolded the note and read it. Another poem.

Roses are red.
Your eyes are blue.

What I'll do if you go,
I haven't a clue.

—B.C.

The gesture was touching, but it still didn't tell her what she needed to know. If she was to judge by his verse, she'd conclude that he didn't want her to leave solely because of the show. That he didn't want to lose his chef.

Jillian closed her eyes. If she was to judge by his actions recently—and they had been quite brotherly—she would conclude that his personal feelings had little to do with his poetic pleas. Or was he using this tactic because she'd insisted on keeping things platonic? Still, she couldn't help but wonder if those notes were only a business gesture on his part.

But she had to be certain. Perhaps if she came right out and told him that she couldn't sleep for thinking of him, that all other men paled in comparison to him, and that she often smiled in private whenever she thought of something he'd done or said, then he'd confess his true feelings for her. Then again, she couldn't imagine baring her soul that way. The wall around her heart was tumbling down, brick by brick, but it still wasn't completely demolished.

The next day, she received two more poems. The first, which she found rolled up and tucked into her coffee cup, read:

Roses are red.
In Texas they're yellow.
Please don't leave
This Boondock fellow.

—B.C.

She found the next one on her car's windshield as she was preparing to drive home that evening. He wasn't much of a poet, but the message gave her reason for hope:

Roses are red,
You look good in pink.
Please meet me tonight;
Let's have a drink.

—B.C.

At the bottom, he had scrawled 8:00 and the name of a nearby restaurant. Jillian excitedly drove home, thinking of the pink dress she would wear for Bill. Maybe tonight he would utter the words she needed to hear.

At home Jillian went for a quick workout in the gym. She was always more clearheaded after exercise, and around Bill she needed all the help she could get.

She had just finished showering, dressing and primping when the doorbell rang. She opened the door to Bill, who handed her a small bouquet of mixed flowers. He was wearing his "wooing suit."

Jillian remembered with dismay the last time he'd worn this suit. It was for his appointment with Susan, when they had discussed the station's ratings and image. She wondered if he considered this a business meeting as well. She couldn't bear the thought, so she switched to another subject.

"I thought we were going to meet at the restaurant."

"The atmosphere down at the Slip is better." His gaze raked over her. "And someone as pretty as you shouldn't be going downtown alone at night, so I thought we could go together. Are you ready?"

Jillian put the flowers in a vase, keeping out a dark pink rosebud to pin to her dress. The addition didn't go unnoticed by Bill, who smiled his approval. In a matter of minutes, they were in the historic Shockoe Slip area of downtown Richmond. They crossed the cobblestone street to one of the renovated warehouses that now held restaurants and night spots for the city's yuppie elite and tourists. Inside, the noise from the bar was almost deafening.

Bill murmured something to the woman at the guest desk, who directed them to the second level. As they took the slow, cagelike elevator up, Jillian couldn't help but notice how comfortable Bill seemed in this setting. He seemed as much at ease here in the brass-and-Tiffany atmosphere as he had at the community-center square dance outside Fullerton.

They were led to a private table near the indoor balcony where they could watch the goings-on downstairs yet still enjoy the relative quiet upstairs.

Bill made small talk until their drinks arrived. Then he bluntly came to the point. "Have you made up your mind about the job offer yet?"

"I promised you I'd wait until Thursday. You still have time to persuade me to stay." *Tell me you love me, and I'll turn them down tonight.*

Bill ran a finger through the moisture on his glass and watched, fascinated, when a droplet trickled down the side. "As you know, I'm not a very eloquent man—"

That's all the more reason to love you.

"—and I'm not the Alan Alda type who can express how deeply I care about something. So I hope this will tell just how much I need you."

Jillian took the slip of paper he pushed across the table.

"By the way," he said, "I made C's in English and literature, so don't expect Browning."

Jillian smiled and unfolded the note.

Roses are red.
Sometimes they're violet.
If you take their offer,
I'll surely cry a lot.

—B.C.

Jillian's smile turned upside down. She hadn't expected anything the caliber of Elizabeth Barrett Browning, but she had thought his expression of caring would be more personal than this. When she thought about what he'd said, she knew he couldn't be referring to his personal feelings.

He had confessed how difficult it was to express how deeply he cared about *something*. The show?

And he had mentioned how much he *needed* her. As the chef to host the program?

"I know it isn't very good," Bill said, "but I didn't expect a frown like that. Is something wrong?"

Jillian was silent as she fished through her purse for a pen. Turning his note over, she scrawled on the back and handed it to him. It was a silly game they were playing, but it was easier to write without trembling than to say what was on her mind without having a catch in her voice.

Softly Bill read the rhyme.

"Roses are red,
Just like my eyes.
Isn't there more between us
Than just baking some pies?

—J.R."

He lifted his eyes from the paper to meet her questioning gaze. "Of course there is. Jillian, no one could ever take your place. We have a rapport—there's a special chemistry between us."

"So you're talking about the show again," she said softly. "Are you trying to talk me into staying for the sake of the ratings?"

"No, I'm trying to tell you that I think it's stupid for us to wait two or three years when we care about each other *now*. We can't lie to our viewers about this attraction between us, and we've got to stop lying to ourselves."

"Viewers?" It all came back to that? She knew Bill would never use her affection as leverage to get her to stay. He was too aboveboard and honest for that. But how much of his interest in her was professional and how much was personal?

"Since we're talking in rhymes and riddles tonight, I've got one more for you." Despite his questionable tactics, she had to know whether his attraction was fleeting or something deeper. "Roses are red," she began, "but there's a hook. Do you want the girl, Or do you want the cook?"

"You're pretty good on the spur of the moment," he told her. "It took me an hour to write each of mine." Reaching across the table, he took her hand in his. "I want *you*, Jillian Reed. I want you beside me at work each day, and I want you beside me in bed each night."

Her throat tightened as his words penetrated her brain. Her heart soared as she realized he was, in an indirect way, professing his desire for her. But he hadn't actually said it. How could she make him realize that she needed to hear those three magic words, without any prompting from her?

"Bill, if you'd told me that before we came back from Fullerton and learned about my other job offer, I would have been thrilled. But now..." Her voice trailed off, and she blinked back a tear. "Now it sounds like you're trying to get me to stay—at least partly—for the sake of the station. How do I know what you really mean when, in the same breath that you say you want me in your bed, you also say you want me at the station?"

"What I was *trying* to say—" Bill braced his hand against the table's edge "—is that I love you, and I can't stand the thought of losing you."

Quietly, tentatively, she ventured, "I love you, too, Bill. But I need to know..."

Oh, how could she tell him she needed to know that it wouldn't be like it had been with Quint? Sure, Quint had loved her in his own way, but he had also seen her as a useful business acquisition. A lover by night, plus a built-in caterer by day to give lavish parties and thus further his career.

Bill had too much integrity to intentionally do the same, but Jillian had to know he was motivated purely by love, both consciously and subconsciously.

"Maybe we should talk about this later, when we're thinking more clearly." She stood and shrugged on her coat. "Thank you for the drink. Don't bother getting up. I can take a taxi home."

Bill stood, almost toppling the chair behind him. "I want to *marry* you, dammit!"

Jillian stopped in the aisle, blocking the path of the waiter. She moved aside for him to pass, but he remained frozen, his eyes fixed on her, just as a dozen other eyes watched her, waiting for her reply. Someone whispered, "Aren't they Boondock Bill and Jill?"

The image of Bill's teetering chair flashed Jillian's thoughts back to his parents' home in Fullerton, where Bill had struggled with Memphis for the last biscuit. She supposed the possibility of losing her kiss to Memphis had prompted him to compete for the biscuit. Had his competitiveness prompted him to propose?

Her eyes filled with burning moisture. "Please don't play games with me," she whispered.

She turned and fled, passing the quaint little elevator and taking the stairs instead, stopping only when she reached the pay phone in the lobby. She didn't bother looking up the taxi company's number in the phone book. She couldn't have read it through the blur.

Catching a flash of pink at the bottom of her eye as she waited for the operator to give her the number, Jillian remembered planning to wear the color for Bill.

Reaching up, she touched the rose, her fingers gently caressing the delicate petals. She was so confused, her thoughts seemed to be whirling. She needed time alone to think. She needed to be away from Bill because he was at the vortex of the whirlpool in her mind.

The recorded voice was calling out the number when the receiver was lifted from her hand and replaced on the hook. Before she could protest, Bill grabbed her hand and led her toward the door.

Jillian pulled back. "What are you doing?"

"Taking you home." He set his jaw, tucked her hand in the crook of his elbow, and again propelled her outside. This time, Jillian didn't resist.

"I could have taken a taxi."

"I wasn't raised that way," he said firmly. "If I take a girl out, I also take her home." She needed time to think. But around him, she was only more confused.

Neither spoke during the drive home. At the apartment, Bill walked Jillian to her door, but she didn't invite him in.

He touched her cheek in a gesture that made Jillian want to forget her career, forget all the reasons she shouldn't—couldn't—marry him.

"What do I have to do," he asked, "to convince you I'm sincere about wanting to marry you?"

Jillian knew that, at this point, anything he did would be too little, too late. If only the job offer had come *after* his proposal. "God knows, I wish I had the answer. I would love to just say yes, but there's so much more I need to think about—that we *both* need to consider. I hope you understand." She touched the dimple in his chin. "Good night."

Not until after she'd closed the door did Jillian allow the tears to come. She sobbed hard, forcing the salty liquid out of her system. Maybe the misery that filled her soul would flow out with the torrent.

Jillian dreaded going back to work Monday. They had crossed over a line and could never go back to the easy camaraderie they had shared before. Regardless of her desire to base her decision on a definite career plan, Jillian knew she now had only one option.

She picked up the phone and dialed Bill's home number. His recorded greeting advised her to leave a message after the beep. Slowly, deliberately, she gave him her decision. "Roses are red. I'm calling to say—" Jillian drew a deep breath to still the tremble in her voice before continuing. "I'll start my new job in two weeks and a day."

Jillian wiped her eyes one last time. From now on she would look only forward—to the pleasure of living in a big city once again, and to all the opportunities that awaited her in Washington. Odd, but now she remembered big cities as cold and lonely places.

Carefully she steered her thoughts away from the welcoming atmosphere of the small town she'd recently visited.

Don't look back, she reminded herself.

If Bill had as rough a weekend as she had, he certainly didn't show it. If anything, he seemed spunkier and more playful than before. Jillian began to wonder if he had received her message on his answering machine. She knew he had when he asked if she'd called the Cooking Institute with her decision and then reminded her of her promise to wait until Thursday to contact them. That was the only time his countenance darkened. His spirits immediately lifted again when she assured him she would not go back on her promise.

Even if she had planned to call before Thursday, she doubted she could make herself dial the number. Although her plans were set, she had no desire to hurry them along. In fact, she'd spent the entire day Saturday helping Lydia cook for and serve the homeless to take her mind off this mess.

When she'd finally returned home after cleaning up Saint Dominick's, she was so exhausted she fell into a dreamless sleep. But not until after she checked the answering machine for a message from Bill. There was none, which reinforced her belief that she had chosen the right course.

Sunday was no better. After sitting through a sermon about love and trust, she threw herself into categorizing her recipes, and then followed with a grueling workout.

And, as if to mock her in her misery, Bill showed up at work Monday, happy as a lark. She had no idea he could be so callous.

Jillian was setting up her ingredients and props for Monday's first taping session when Memphis entered the studio with Darlene at his heels. The young program editor seemed to be helping him hide something behind his broad back.

"Miss Jillian!" Memphis boomed.

Jillian jumped.

Memphis withdrew six flawless yellow roses from behind him and presented them to her. Darlene beamed.

"What's this for?" Her first thought was of Bill's poem that mentioned yellow roses and ended, "Please don't leave this Boondock fellow." Had he solicited their help to get her to change her mind?

"Congratulations!" Memphis continued in his booming voice.

Mike left his camera and shook her hand. "We're real happy for you, Jillian."

"Aren't you excited?" Darlene gushed.

"Look," said Jillian, "I don't know what Bill told you, but whatever it was, he's sadly mistaken."

"What do you mean, mistaken?" demanded Darlene. Turning to Memphis, she grabbed his sleeve and pulled until he faced her. "The show *has* been syndicated, hasn't it?"

Memphis tugged a handful of beard. "Yeah. I saw the letter myself on Friday."

"Syndicated?" By now, Jill was really confused.

"Didn't Bill tell you?" Memphis asked.

"No, he—"

Friday. The same day he'd proposed to her. If there'd been any doubt before, it was gone now. Bill *had* been motivated by profit.

"—he was very busy that day."

"I don't see how he could have been too busy to mention something like that," the editor grumbled.

Jillian gently took the roses from Memphis. "Never mind that," she told them both. "Your good wishes are very dear to me. I'm going to put these beautiful flowers in a vase on the counter so our viewers can enjoy them, too."

When Bill arrived on the set, he was scolded by Memphis, Darlene, and even the usually silent cameraman.

Jillian didn't scold him, but she had to ask, out of earshot of the others, "Why didn't you tell me?"

"As you might recall," he responded dryly, "I had something else on my mind that day."

"Like trying to keep me from messing up the syndication deal?"

"Is that what you think?"

"What else could I think?"

"You're a hard one to convince, aren't you?"

It was hard to keep her mind on the recipe for Spanish rice, but Bill seemed unaffected by the tension that flowed between them. After they cooked the rice, she spooned it onto a plate. Bill grabbed a rose from the arrangement, clamped it between his teeth, and performed a bizarre version of the flamenco dance.

He continued with his Boondock Bill mischief for the next two days. With one more day before she was to call the institute, Jillian's anxiety grew. And so did Bill's silliness. By Wednesday afternoon, she'd had about all she could take of his disregard for her feelings.

He insisted on making butterscotch pudding while she prepared the Penne Bake.

"Why don't you call it Macaroni Bake?" he taunted. "No one knows what Penne is."

Jillian's patience snapped. "Why don't you concentrate on your pudding!"

"No need to get testy." Then he hummed a cheerful tune until she told him to knock it off. "When my little sister got cranky like that, my mother always made her get more sleep. Maybe you should go to bed earlier," he offered helpfully. "I'd be happy to tuck you in."

"I don't wish to discuss my sleeping habits on this show," Jillian said through gritted teeth.

"Okay, but don't say I didn't try to help."

He lifted a spoonful of the warm pudding to her mouth. "Here, try this. It'll make you feel better."

"I haven't finished the Penne yet. And we usually do the tasting at the end of the show."

"I put a secret ingredient in it," he urged, pushing the spoon at her. "Watch out for the crunchy part."

Jillian accepted the pudding from the overloaded spoon. Swallowing, she felt something hard go down. She put her hand to her throat. "What was that?"

"You found the crunchy part? Great. Now spit it out."

"I swallowed it!" She clutched his shirtsleeve. "What did I just swallow?"

"You *ate* the surprise ingredient?"

"Of course I did! What did you expect me to do with it?"

"You were just supposed to notice it."

Jillian couldn't imagine what he might have put in the pudding or why. She began to suspect it might be part of a kitchen utensil. But why would he do that? "Bill, what did you put in that pudding?"

"Don't panic, but I think you'd better come with me." He unclipped the microphone from his collar and then started removing hers.

"Don't panic! What do you mean, don't panic? Did you poison me?"

Bill shook his head. Taking her hand, he started leading her out of the studio. "Mike, we're going to the emergency room."

Mike shrugged as if this were an ordinary event. He unfastened the camera from its tripod, attached a battery pack to his belt, and followed them out the door.

The next hour, Jillian's moods swung from fear that she might die from whatever she'd swallowed, to annoyance that Bill would purposely put something in her pudding, to anger that he wouldn't tell her what it was.

While she changed into a paper gown, Bill talked quietly with the doctor. She overheard Dr. Pishdad's response from behind the privacy screen when he informed Bill that, in a case like this, she wouldn't need to have her stomach pumped.

She had her abdomen X-rayed. Jillian was grateful when the technician escorted Bill and Mike away from the X-ray room. She'd been tempted to clunk them both over the head with Mike's camera.

Afterward she changed back into her clothes and followed Dr. Pishdad to his office. Although he was smiling broadly, she didn't see what was so funny about having Mike trail them with his camera.

She and Bill sat in the two guest chairs across the desk from the doctor while Mike maneuvered to a prime filming spot at the side of the room.

"Does he have to do that?" she asked Bill.

"Just ignore him."

Dr. Pishdad cleared his throat and commanded their attention. "I have your X-ray, and it appears that the foreign object should pass without medical intervention. Come back in a couple of days, and I'll check you again to make sure there are no complications."

He stood and walked to the light screen on the wall near his desk. "I'll turn on the light so you can examine your X-ray," he told Jillian. "And then I believe Mr. Clayton has something to say to you."

With a sly smile at Bill, Dr. Pishdad flipped the switch and moved to the back of the room.

Mike positioned his camera on the light screen.

The outline of Jillian's ribs and vertebrae glowed white against the black film. She stood up and walked closer. In the soft tissue, under the rib cage and to one side of the backbone, Jillian could make out the image of a small circular object.

She became aware of Bill beside her. "It wasn't supposed to happen like this," he told her. "We did most of our courting on the show, and it seemed only fitting that I ask you to marry me in front of the viewers who've watched us fall in love. But I guess the ring in the pudding wasn't such a great idea."

She turned to look at the man who'd put her through so much in the past hour...in the past weeks. There was no hint of teasing in his eyes.

"I want you to marry me."

"Bill," she said softly, "we've been through this before..." Did he think that, by having witnesses, he could pressure her into staying?

"Yes, we have. But this time I want to make sure you know why I'm asking you to be my wife." He grasped both her arms but didn't hold her. "I love you, Jillian, and I want you near me always. I wanted to tell you this sooner. If I'd been smarter, I would have listened to the fortune-teller's advice and told you then how much I love you. When it looked as though you might take that position on the cooking school's faculty, I knew I couldn't let you go."

Jillian wanted to believe him. She really did. Bill was all she had ever hoped for in a husband, and more. He was loving and fun, and she knew he'd be a wonderful and doting father, as well. She honestly believed that he loved her, but she couldn't help wondering how much his proposal was spurred by the fear of losing the chef of one of his station's top-rated shows.

Before she could express her misgivings, Bill extracted two pieces of paper from his pocket.

"I have a couple of engagement gifts for you." He handed her a photo. "I'm looking at this piece of property in Powhatan—it's a rural county a little farther out than the station. The property has a nice big house, a catfish pond, and thirty-four acres of land. That's plenty of room for both of us, a couple of kids and Frank. And look, there's a clothesline in the backyard. I won't have to hang my underwear on the deer's antlers anymore."

"This is all very nice, but—"

"And here, as you would say, is the pièce de résistance." Bill unfolded a document with a flourish.

Jillian examined the legal form. "A rental agreement for space in the shopping center across from the station?"

"Not just any rental agreement." He pointed to paragraph eleven. "It's a lease for kitchen and classroom space, and it's contingent upon your approval.

You could run your own cooking school and write a cookbook in your spare time. Jillian,'' he said, loving her with his eyes in a way that made her wish they were back on Lookout Rock, "I don't care if you leave the show, just as long as you don't leave me.''

Jillian had thought she'd steeled herself to Bill's proposal, but his thoughtfulness was her undoing.

Looking into his earnest gray-green eyes, she knew, without a doubt, he held no surprises up his sleeve and that this was not just a scheme to keep her on the popular cooking program.

She had misjudged him, not once but several times, and he had proved her wrong each time. She now knew that behind that funny, drawling accent was an intelligent man with a college degree. And, because of the incident with Belinda, she knew him to be an honest and just man.

But, most of all, she knew he was a man of integrity—a man she could trust. A man, she had come to realize, she could love unreservedly.

"Marry me, Jillian.''

Jillian stepped into his arms and kissed him, oblivious to the camera that recorded it all.

"Yes, Bill, if you'll still have me.''

He took her in his embrace, enveloping her in his love.

Jillian had finally found her roots.

Epilogue

Jillian's mother helped her dress for this most important taping of the newly named "Plain 'N' Fancy Cooking" show. Her father was sitting in the studio with Jillian's grandmother, waiting for the proceedings to begin.

"Maybe you should change into your gown *after* you frost the wedding cake. If I were you, I certainly wouldn't want to get sugar on this beautiful white dress."

"Bill insisted," Jillian told her mother. Her parents had warmed to Bill immediately, but it would take them a while to get used to his unorthodox ways. After all, even Jillian had needed some time to adjust to him.

A lot had happened in the month and a half since Bill proposed to her in the emergency room.

Jillian spread her fingers as she admired the large diamond on her left hand. She had experienced a moment's hesitation that day when Bill had asked her to wear his ring. Fortunately he had quickly assured her that the ring he'd placed in the pudding had been a cheap stand-in since he'd expected she would want to select the real thing herself.

Renovations would soon be complete on her new cooking school, and she would begin teaching her first class after she and Bill were finished with this season's filmings. Jillian had been the one to insist on continuing with the show. She couldn't bear to lose the very thing that had brought her and Bill together in the first place. And, by taping several segments a day, they could do a year's worth of shows in just a few months. The rest of her time would be spent teaching at her new school and working on a cookbook. Thanks to Susan's suggestion, Jillian and Bill were also scheduled to make public appearances at a shopping mall and the grand opening of a new grocery store, as well as conduct a seminar for a senior-citizens group.

Bill had touched her with his generosity and thoughtfulness when he had called the director of the soup kitchen and offered to donate the food they prepared each day to the homeless. He had also urged Jillian to do the same with the surplus from her cooking school.

"I still don't think it's a good idea for the groom to see the bride before the actual ceremony begins," her mother fussed.

"Believe me, Mother, our segment of the cooking show will be part of the ceremony."

The elder Ms. Reed sniffed. "It seems as though your wedding ceremony will be part of the cooking show."

Jillian laughed. "It should be quite memorable. Besides," she added, recalling Bill's very words, "it seems only fair that since our viewers watched us fall in love, they should be welcome at the wedding."

All talking ceased as they entered the studio. Jillian smiled at the loving faces of the people who had come to witness the wedding. Her grandmother was seated beside her father, and Jillian hugged them both. Bill's parents and sister were there, and so were Mrs. Preston, Memphis and many of the employees of WXYZ. And Belinda had sought her out earlier to announce her promotion to the position of relief cook. Jillian was glad to hear that the teen had told the Claytons the truth behind the disappearance of Jillian's recipe cards.

Jillian took her place beside Bill at the cooking island. Having already baked and cooled the cake layers, she assembled them and demonstrated how to decorate it. When that was done, she mixed a batch of Bride's Punch.

True to form, Bill couldn't resist a little teasing. "When the honeymoon's over," he advised the audience, "it's called Wife's Punch...to be served with Husband's Duck."

Jillian laughed again and thought how she'd laughed more since she'd met Bill than she had in all the rest of her life.

He was handsome in his tuxedo. She couldn't help wishing away the remainder of the day so she could help him out of it. It was hard to imagine she had once been too blind to see how truly wonderful Bill Clayton was.

"I don't expect us to fight," she commented, "but you have to admit we make an unlikely combination."

Taking her in his arms, Bill kissed her and said, "We have the best recipe of all: love, laughter, and respect— a lovin' spoonful of each."

* * * * *

**HE'S MORE THAN
A MAN, HE'S
ONE OF OUR**

UNCLE DADDY

Kasey Michaels

Gabe Logan was doing just fine raising his orphaned niece
alone. He didn't need or *want* any help from the baby's aunt,
Erica Fletcher. Gabe could see that the uptight businesswoman
didn't have a clue about child rearing. So when Erica
suggested Gabe teach her about parenting, it was an offer he
couldn't resist. Having her move into his house would surely
force Erica to admit defeat. But when she set out to conquer his
heart . . . Gabe knew he was in big trouble!

Find out the true meaning of *close quarters* in Kasey Michaels's
UNCLE DADDY, available in February.

Fall in love with our **Fabulous Fathers**—and join the Silhouette
Romance family!

FF293

**Three All-American beauties discover
love comes in all shapes and sizes!**

ALL-AMERICAN SWEETHEARTS

by Laurie Paige

CARA'S BELOVED (#917)—*February*

SALLY'S BEAU (#923)—*March*

VICTORIA'S CONQUEST (#933)—*April*

A lost love, a new love and a hidden one, three
All-American Sweethearts get their men in Paradise Falls,
West Virginia. Only in America...and only
from Silhouette Romance!

Silhouette
R O M A N C E™

Silhouette
R O M A N C E™

HEARTLAND HOLIDAYS

**Christmas bells turn into wedding bells for the Gallagher
siblings in Stella Bagwell's *Heartland Holidays* trilogy.**

THEIR FIRST THANKSGIVING (#903) in November
Olivia Westcott had once rejected Sam Gallagher's proposal—
and in his stubborn pride, he'd refused to hear her reasons why.
Now Olivia is back...and it is about time Sam Gallagher listened!

THE BEST CHRISTMAS EVER (#909) in December
Soldier Nick Gallagher had come home to be the best man at his
brother's wedding—not to be a groom! But when he met single
mother Allison Lee, he knew he'd found his bride.

NEW YEAR'S BABY (#915) in January
Kathleen Gallagher had given up on love and marriage until she
came to the rescue of neighbor Ross Douglas . . . and the newborn
baby he'd found on his doorstep!

Come celebrate the holidays with Silhouette Romance!

Silhouette SPECIAL EDITION

It takes a very special man to win

That **SPECIAL** *Woman!*

She's friend, wife, mother—she's you! And beside each Special Woman stands a wonderfully *special* man. It's a celebration of our heroines—and the men who become part of their lives.

Look for these exciting titles from Silhouette Special Edition:

January   **BUILDING DREAMS** by Ginna Gray

February   **HASTY WEDDING** by Debbie Macomber

March   **THE AWAKENING** by Patricia Coughlin

April   **FALLING FOR RACHEL** by Nora Roberts

Dont miss THAT SPECIAL WOMAN! each month—from your special authors.

AND

For the most special woman of all—you, our loyal reader—we have a wonderful gift: a beautiful journal to record all of your special moments. See this month's THAT SPECIAL WOMAN! title for details.

TSW1

Stevenson

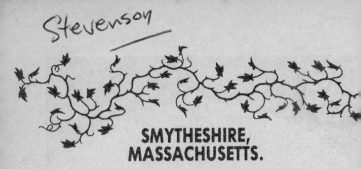

SMYTHESHIRE, MASSACHUSETTS.

Small town. Big secrets.

**Silhouette Romance invites you to visit Elizabeth August's
small town, a place with a legacy rooted deep
in the past....**

THE VIRGIN WIFE
February 1993
Madaline MacGreggor-Smythe lived a far-from-ordinary exis-
tence. Though married, she had never experienced romantic intimacy and probably never would. But when Colin Darnell—a man
from Madaline's past—returns to town, feelings long denied are
rekindled. And so is the danger that had separated them!

HAUNTED HUSBAND
March 1993—FABULOUS FATHERS
Thatcher Brant, widower and father of two, vowed never to love
again. This chief of police would not risk his feelings, or those of
his children, for anyone. Least of all, Samantha Hogan. But
something had told Samantha that Thatcher was the husband
for her!

SMYTHESHIRE, MASSACHUSETTS—this sleepy little town has
plenty to keep you up at night. Only from Silhouette Romance!

Silhouette
R O M A N C E™

SREA1